MW01136675

SHARING THE MIRACLE

THE RIVER RAIN SERIES
BOOK 5.5

KRISTEN ASHLEY

Sharing the Miracle

Sharing the Miracle

A River Rain Novel

By Kristen Ashley

Copyright 2023 Kristen Ashley

ISBN: 978-1-957568-97-3

Published by Blue Box Press, an imprint of Evil Eye Concepts, Incorporated

All rights reserved. No part of this book may be reproduced, scanned, or distributed in any printed or electronic form without permission. Please do not participate in or encourage piracy of copyrighted materials in violation of the author's rights.

This is a work of fiction. Names, places, characters and incidents are the product of the author's imagination and are fictitious. Any resemblance to actual persons, living or dead, events or establishments is solely coincidental.

BOOK DESCRIPTION

Sharing the Miracle
A River Rain Novella
By Kristen Ashley

From *New York Times* bestselling author Kristen Ashley comes a new novella in her River Rain Series...

Elsa Cohen has everything she ever wanted.

A challenging career. A bicoastal lifestyle.

And an amazing man—the kind, loving and handsome Hale Wheeler—who adores her and has asked her to be his wife.

She isn't ready for the surprise news she's received.

And she doesn't know how to tell Hale.

Once Hale discovers that his future has taken a drastic turn, a fear he's never experienced takes hold.

He just doesn't understand why.

Family and friends rally around the couple as they adjust to their new reality, and along the way, more surprises hit the River Rain crew as love is tested and life goes on.

ABOUT KRISTEN ASHLEY

Kristen Ashley is the *New York Times* bestselling author of over eighty romance novels including the *Rock Chick, Colorado Mountain, Dream Man, Chaos, Unfinished Heroes, The 'Burg, Magdalene, Fantasyland, The Three, Ghost and Reincarnation, Moonlight and Motor Oil, Dream Team, River Rain* and *Honey* series along with several standalone novels. She's a hybrid author, publishing titles both independently and traditionally, her books have been translated in fourteen languages and she's sold over five million books.

Kristen's novel, *Law Man*, won the *RT Book Reviews* Reviewer's Choice Award for best Romantic Suspense. Her independently published title *Hold On* was nominated for *RT Book Reviews* best Independent Contemporary Romance and her traditionally published title *Breathe* was nominated for best Contemporary Romance. Kristen's titles *Motorcycle Man, The Will, Ride Steady* (which won the Reader's Choice award from *Romance Reviews*) and *The Hookup* all made the final rounds for Goodreads Choice Awards in the Romance category.

Kristen, born in Gary and raised in Brownsburg, Indiana, was a fourth-generation graduate of Purdue University. Since, she has lived in Denver, the West Country of England, and now she resides in Phoenix. She worked as a charity executive for eighteen years prior to beginning her independent publishing career. She currently writes full-time.

Although romance is her genre, the prevailing themes running through all of Kristen's novels are friendship, family and a strong sisterhood. To this end, and as a way to thank her readers for their support, Kristen has created the Rock Chick Nation, a series of programs that are designed to give back to her readers and promote a strong female community.

The mission of the Rock Chick Nation is to live your best life, be true to your true self, recognize your beauty and take your sister's back whether they're friends and family or if they're thousands of miles away and you don't know who they are. The programs of the RC Nation include: Rock Chick Rendezvous, weekends Kristen organizes full of parties and get-togethers to bring the sisterhood together; Rock Chick Recharges, evenings Kristen arranges for women who have been nominated to receive a special night; and Rock Chick Rewards, an ongoing program that raises funds for nonprofit women's organizations Kristen's readers nominate. Kristen's Rock Chick Rewards have donated over $180,000 to charity and this number continues to rise.

You can read more about Kristen, her titles and the Rock Chick Nation at KristenAshley.net.

Wildest Dreams

The Golden Dynasty

Fantastical

Broken Dove

Midnight Soul

Gossamer in the Darkness

The Honey Series:

The Deep End

The Farthest Edge

The Greatest Risk

The Magdalene Series:

The Will

Soaring

The Time in Between

Moonlight and Motor Oil Series:

The Hookup

The Slow Burn

The River Rain Series:

After the Climb

Chasing Serenity

Taking the Leap

Making the Match

Fighting the Pull

Sharing the Miracle

Embracing the Change

Other Titles by Kristen Ashley:

Heaven and Hell

Play It Safe

Three Wishes

Complicated

Loose Ends

Fast Lane

Perfect Together

Too Good to Be True

AUTHOR'S ACKNOWLEDGEMENTS

With a cornucopia of food surrounding us, and day drinking the matter at hand, this novella was born.

I loved the idea of telling some sweet short stories in the River Rain world to allow myself to spend more time with these characters and keep my readers up to date with all that's going on.

So, a hearty thank you to Liz Berry for listening to my ramblings, then championing them.

And more gratitude to the entire Blue Box Press Team—Jillian Stein, MJ Rose, Stacey Tardif, Asha Hossein and Kim Guidroz—and my team—Donna Perry and Amanda Simpson—for turning this book around from writing to publishing in a matter of weeks.

As ever, and always, you ladies rock!

AUTHOR'S NOTE

When Elsa and Hale's story, *Fighting the Pull*, came out, I was delighted when a number of my readers noted how they were bummed they had to wait an entire year for another River Rain novel to be released.

Even if I was delighted you all wanted more, I was also troubled, because it would be an entire year before another River Rain novel was released, and I know how hard it is to wait!

At this same time, one of my readers asked a certain question about Hale and Elsa and their future.

As I was talking with Liz, my editor, about the future of River Rain, I had a brainstorm.

The truth was, I really couldn't fit two River Rain novels in my yearly publishing schedule, but I miss them when they're gone too.

So the brainstorm was...why not keep this family going between books with novellas?

That was when this story was born (and, as ever, I have other ideas percolating too!). A chance for me, and my readers, to go back to the River Rain family and see how they live their lives and face life's challenges...together.

I love this. I love it because this series was born of my readers and me building the books together, and in essence, this novella is no different.

Therefore, here you go.

The answer to some questions, the continuation to some stories and a return to River Rain.

I hope you enjoy.

And always remember to Rock On!

CHAPTER 1

GOOD NEWS

Elsa

I messed up.

Again.

As I sat on the edge of the exam table, my legs dangling, my eyes glued to my doctor, I realized, in the haze of falling in love, getting engaged and sorting a new, and hectic, bicoastal life with my fiancé, I'd blown it.

Yes.

Again.

My doctor was studying me intently.

"Is this not good news?" she asked.

Yes.

It was good news.

It was the best news ever.

It was just that I worried Hale wouldn't think of it the same way.

"How did this happen?" I asked. "I'm on the pill."

"Are you taking another medication I don't know about?"

I shook my head.

"Did you by chance miss a dose?"

I shook my head again.

"Do you abstain during fertile periods?"

I bit my lip.

She fought a smile.

Then she shared, "No birth control is foolproof, Elsa." The intensity of her gaze grew grave. "I have to ask again, isn't this good news?"

"It's the best news ever," I told her quietly. "It's just that my fiancé told me he doesn't want children."

She smiled. "I've heard that before, and then something like this happens, and they change their mind."

That might be true for many others.

But Hale hadn't wanted a partner, definitely not to get married.

And here we were.

He hadn't wanted to back off his ambitious and back-breaking goals to save the world.

Now, he shared that mission with his right-hand executive man, Javi, so the goals were still ambitious, but not back-breaking.

And although he was great with kids, and Genny and Tom taught him how to be a good parent, his own mother and father faltered (hugely) in that endeavor, and how that played out had scored marks into his soul. And when that kind of thing happened, it tended to make the child who endured that manner of being raised gun-shy about repeating his or her parent's mistakes.

We'd imploded the last time both of us didn't keep the finger on the pulse of where we were and what we wanted from each other and our future (Hale bore the brunt of that, but I, too, hadn't been communicative with him).

Hale had compromised again and again in our relationship.

And this would be the biggest compromise of them all.

Because...surprise!

I was having his baby.

CHAPTER 2

DIAMONDS

Elsa

The text came in when I was panicking at the same time riding up the elevator to my doom (that doom being somehow, during that short elevator ride, figuring out how to tell Hale I was pregnant with the child he didn't want, then getting out of the elevator and sharing that miracle).

The text was from Tom, and it came into the "family" text string.

By the way, the "family" text string included Mika, Cadence, Genny, Duncan, Sully, Gage, Chloe, Judge, Sasha, Matt, Hale and me.

And this family text string was busy.

I probably received, on average, seven texts a day from one or another member of that string. They ranged from the important, like someone was going to be in town, to the ridiculous, and these were usually hilarious gifs or links to TikToks from Gage, but Chloe was a master gif sender as well.

Sasha, on the other hand, sent Daily Moments of Zen texts with gifs of lapping waves or swimming turtles. Those were not hilarious, but that reminder to take a second to chill out every day was a smart one.

It felt good to be in this company. It felt good, when we were scattered from New York to Arizona to LA, to be in touch every day in some way.

I loved it for me, having my family expanded so exponentially by good, caring (hilarious) people.

I loved it more for Hale, that he had any family at all, and such a great one no less.

However, this text also was sent to an alternate, expanded "family" text string that added Jamie, Nora, Dru, Rix, Alex, Blake and Ned to that list.

That wasn't unheard of, considering Jamie was Judge's dad, Dru was his sister, Rix was his best friend and Nora was Mika's best friend, not to mention Alex was Rix's fiancée, and Blake was her sister, Ned her father.

Still, that string wasn't nearly as busy. It could light up, especially if someone was coming to New York, but it didn't include daily communication.

Though, what made this particular text from Tom highly unusual was that it also included my dad, my mom and my brother and sister.

Actually, that wasn't unusual.

It was bizarre.

It wasn't that my family hadn't been adopted by that extended family. It was just, we were the newest members, so we weren't quite fully in the fold (well, Dad was, and Oskar kind of was, but Mom and Emilie could be difficult to deal with, so they weren't).

Tom's text said: *Important family meeting. In person. Jamie's house. Clear your calendars for Saturday afternoon at 2:00.*

"What on earth?" I whispered as the elevator doors to Hale's and my fabulous Manhattan penthouse opened.

I saw what I usually saw if Hale was home before me.

My handsome fiancé sauntering my way with a smile on his face.

For a moment, I lost my anxiety, because, from the time he ambushed me at my old studio in Brooklyn a year ago, the first time we'd ever had a face-to-face conversation, to now, this man walking toward me was a changed man.

When I first met him he'd been alternately pugnacious and flirtatious, but underneath, standoffish was always simmering.

The man who was coming my way was a man content, at peace with his life, his relationship, his work and his family, and he let that show openly on his face.

I'd had a hand in that, and I was a big-deal celebrity interviewer making seven figures before the age of thirty. Even so, that look on Hale's face was my proudest achievement.

And...

Damn.

I was about to blow it to smithereens.

My phone in my hand vibrated with another text, but I was engaged with walking out of the elevator and tipping my head back to get my nightly kiss from Hale.

Though, as I did it, I noted we had surprise company.

Chloe and Judge were there.

And this was a big surprise, since they didn't stop by from their place in Tribeca. They didn't live in Tribeca.

They lived in Prescott, Arizona.

Therefore I got my kiss, Hale gave me his sweet, quiet, "Hey, baby." I gave him the same in return. And only then did I turn my attention to Hale's sister-from-another-sister-and-mister and his brother-in-law.

"This is a nice surprise," I greeted, thinking, *Actually, a nice reprieve.*

But although I had a reprieve, I didn't have relief, because, unlike being in denial and procrastinating on having the conversation I'd needed to have with Hale all those months ago about where our relationship was heading, which led to four of the worst days of my entire life when I thought he'd broken up with me, this one wasn't one I'd be able to avoid. Eventually, it would make its presence known, and I needed to have tackled it *way* before that happened.

I walked in and threw my attaché on the couch just in time to get a hug and cheek touch from Chloe, and the same, but with a cheek kiss from Judge.

They were already drinking cocktails.

Hale, as was usual with Hale, noticed me eyeing the glasses on the coffee table.

"Judge and I are on martinis. Chloe, a cosmo. Want one?" he asked. "Or a glass of wine?"

Shit, shit, shit.

"I've got a nagging headache, nothing big, but I'm going to lay off the alcohol for tonight," I lied.

And great.

Already lying.

My phone still in my hand vibrated again with another text.

I ignored it in order to bend and give love to Frosty, our cat, who'd come up to say hi.

Cheddar, our other cat, wasn't to be seen, which meant, even if he no longer looked like a kitten, he was somewhere behaving like a kitten.

In other words, getting into trouble.

"Want some ibuprofen, or Excedrin?" Hale asked, his eyes narrowed on me in concern.

But I had my own concern.

Could I take that stuff anymore?

I had a bunch of leaflets in my attaché as given to me by my doctor. I also had a follow-up appointment next week to talk to her about what to expect the next seven months, an appointment she urged me to bring Hale to.

But in the meantime, as a priority, I had to find time to read them.

However, since I didn't actually have a headache, just a percolating infant in my womb, I was forced to lie again.

"I took some earlier. It's already working. I'll be good soon."

"I'll get you some water," he muttered as he moved toward the kitchen.

I shrugged off my coat, threw it over the arm of an armchair and collapsed into it.

I was about to ask what brought Chloe and Judge to New York, when I noticed something in all that was taking up my headspace that I hadn't noticed before.

Something was off with Chloe.

And as such, something was off with Judge, but only in the sense he seemed to have a weird vibe that was emanating toward Chloe.

How I knew this, I didn't know, because I was getting to know both of them more and more, but we weren't best buds (yet).

Perhaps I'd honed it through my career that started when I interviewed my dad when I was in single digits and never let up. Perhaps it was from my habit of people watching. Perhaps it was a bit of both.

But...*wait.*

I kept studying them, and...

Oh my.

Maybe Chloe was pregnant too.

I loved that for the little tyke I was playing host to, a cousin their age would be awesome.

And I loved that for Chloe and Judge, who would be great parents.

I still had a mammoth hurdle to jump in my own situation.

"So what brings you two to New York?" I asked belatedly.

Oddly, Chloe didn't answer. Instead, she gave me big eyes which I was certain I was supposed to be able to read, but alas, as we weren't best buds (yet), I could not.

Therefore, I gave them back.

She returned them again, before jerking her chin toward the kitchen, meaning Hale.

My heart lurched.

Was something up with Hale?

Nothing seemed up with Hale.

Had I misread my man?

Did this have to do with the text from Tom?

"What?" I mouthed.

She shook her head in the negative, barely perceptible, and I knew why.

A glass of water came into my line of vision, offered to me by my guy.

I took it with a, "Thanks, honey."

He sat on the arm of my chair that wasn't holding my coat just as another text came in.

Maybe all the texting was what Chloe's gestures were about.

Curious as ever, even if my life—after five positive drugstore tests, and a credentialed medical doctor confirming—was unexpectedly derailed, I picked up my phone from my thigh and turned it over just as Hale answered the question neither Chloe nor Judge did, "They got advance notice of that text Tom just sent and headed out early so Judge and I could get some work done and Chloe could get some shopping done."

"I'm meeting with two designers who I might stock at my stores, Hale," Chloe drawled petulantly, something she was really good at when it came to Hale.

Then again, he was the older brother who gave her shit constantly, so she'd had practice.

Hale grinned at her and teased, "And shopping."

See?

"Of course. I *am* me," she returned.

As this happened, I saw the first text was from Genny, the second from Sully, and while I was studying my phone, a third one came in from Rix.

I didn't read them, but I sensed what they were about.

It was Thursday evening.

Demanding an in-person family meeting in New York, when quite a few of the people who were attending were on the West Coast, with not even two days of notice was not only inconvenient, it was concerning.

"Is everything all right with Tom?" I asked Hale.

"I don't know," Hale replied. "I just know my plane left two hours ago to do the rounds of picking everybody up."

What?

Whoa!

I turned to Chloe and Judge. "Do you know what's going on?"

Judge shook his head and said, "No clue."

Chloe added, "Dad just said it wasn't bad."

"Are you worried?" I asked her.

"What I'm hoping is that it's an intervention between Jamie and Nora," she responded.

Instantly, I was hoping that too.

Jamie and Nora had been pussyfooting around each other for *ages*. They spent more time together than most husbands and wives, and yet they lived apart and kept calling each other "friends" and "companions" when everyone could tell Nora was in deep for Jamie, and the only one who didn't know Jamie was in deep for Nora was Nora... and Jamie.

"What I suspect is that Dad and Mika are going to announce they're engaged," Chloe went on.

Suddenly, my mood took an upswing.

"Oh my God, that'd be brilliant!" I cried.

Chloe smiled, it was genuine.

It was still...*off.*

"I know," she replied.

"Not sure I get the drama," Hale muttered.

I glanced up at him to see he wasn't angry or upset. That said, we were some of the ones for whom this wasn't inconvenient seeing as we lived in the city.

"I love the drama," Chloe put in, unsurprisingly.

"You love that it's an excuse for all of us to get together," Judge amended.

"That as well," Chloe replied.

They stared at each other for a beat, then two, then three, and this was as strange as everything else that was happening that evening, because they were communicating, they just weren't speaking.

"So we're here for that," Judge began, aiming those words to Chloe, then he looked toward us. "But also..."

He didn't finish.

He was back to staring at his wife.

She fidgeted in her seat on the couch.

"Baby," Judge prompted.

"Maybe after dinner," she murmured. "And about three more cocktails."

"Maybe get it out of the way," Judge returned.

"Maybe don't push," she shot back, becoming noticeably agitated.

"Maybe we've been having this discussion for the last six months and you need to stop procrastinating," Judge retorted.

"We're all family here, and we're all friends," Hale cut in. "So this is a safe space for you to share whatever it is you two are talking about."

My man.

He had a way.

And that way was just telling them to spill it already without using those words.

"Hale—" Chloe started, but she cut herself off, a sudden acute look of worry on her face.

I tensed even as I felt Hale tense beside me.

"What?" Hale asked, his voice sharper with concern. "Are you okay?"

"She's fine. We're fine. Everyone is fine," Judge assured. "It's just that we noticed something off about our wedding rings."

Um...

Hunh?

Hale sounded as confused as I felt. "Your wedding rings?"

"Yes, we noticed it right away, on our wedding day, the minute we slipped them on each other's fingers," Chloe stated. "I thought Judge did it. He thought I did. When we talked about it and found out neither of us was responsible, we thought maybe it was a mistake by the jeweler. But when we got back from our honeymoon, I called the jeweler, and she said the alterations to our rings were ordered by..." Now that acute worry she was reflecting was joined by acute discomfort before she finished, "Rhys."

That name made Hale's edginess ring the top bell, because Rhys— otherwise known as Corey Szabo's right-hand man, a role he was still playing, even if tragically Corey, Hale's dad, was no longer of this world—had yet to connect with Hale. This was something Hale had requested repeatedly over the last six months, only to be alternately ignored or rebuffed.

In other words, the mysterious Mr. Rhys Vaughn was going to remain a mystery until he decided he wasn't going to be that anymore.

And my man was a control freak in all the good ways.

But for this, it was bad, because he wanted that connection with Rhys mostly because he wanted to understand who the man was to his dead father.

That was something I wanted for him as well, not to mention I felt he was entitled to the knowledge, and that meant I was also getting pretty pissed Rhys was delaying the (I hoped) inevitable.

But Rhys being involved in this meant...

Chloe interrupted my thoughts as she kept speaking.

"The inside of my ring is edged, top and bottom, in little pavé diamonds," she explained. "And Judge's has a large diamond embedded in his."

"And what does Rhys have to do with that?" Hale asked, though he had to know.

"Well," Chloe said slowly. "When we called the jeweler to ask if it was a mistake, even though it's fabulous, a beautiful surprise, just for Judge and me to know they're there—"

"Babe," Judge warned as she got off target.

Chloe cleared her throat and continued, "So, the jeweler said she couldn't wait for us to call and ask, because she was dying to tell us that a Rhys Vaughn came in and ordered the additions. And he told her to tell us when we contacted her that those diamonds, they're... they're..." She drew in a breath, and finished it, "Oh, Hale. Those diamonds are a wedding gift from Uncle Corey."

And there it was.

So, okay.

Now I got why they were acting weird.

To say Hale was raw after he had opened the box his father left him after he committed suicide was a vast understatement.

Since then, he'd been sorting through those feelings with me, Tom, Genny, even Jamie. As such, he was talking about his dad more often.

While he did that, he seemed to be getting past the guilt of not noticing how hard his father tried to be a good dad, and how he hadn't noticed it when Corey was alive.

Through Rhys, Corey, I'd learned, had been doing a lot from beyond the grave since he passed. But we hadn't had anything since Hale opened his box.

Now...this.

I grabbed Hale's hand as I felt the emotion beating off him.

I squeezed it as we all waited for him to share his reaction verbally with us.

And then it came, it came softly, and with so much love, tears pricked the backs of my eyes.

"So Dad." I watched a small, melancholy smile form on his lips. "Drama. Extravagance. And secrecy. All at the same time."

I heard Chloe's quiet sob right before she was up, Hale was also standing, and they were holding each other. Chloe had her face tucked in Hale's chest, and Hale had his sister held tight.

I turned to Judge to see his eyes warm and a small smile playing on his lips while his focus remained on his wife.

Then I looked down at my left ring finger, because Corey had already given Hale and me diamonds. Valuable stones that sparkled, but what was far more precious was the history and love that came with them.

And it was then, not for the first time, and I knew it wouldn't be the last, I felt a wholesale sense of loss that Hale's dad was no longer with us.

And what was worse for me...

I would never have the chance to meet him.

And now, our baby wouldn't either.

IT WAS AFTER WE CAME HOME FROM DINNER.

After I lied again about still being worried about my headache returning and not drinking any alcohol at dinner, or when we got home, and they all had cognac, and I did not.

It was when Chloe and Judge were heading into the biggest and best guest room of several we had, and Hale and I were heading into our room.

That was when Chloe threatened, her voice ringing down the hall, "If you change this fabulous bedroom into a nursery, taking away my sanctuary when I'm in the Big Apple, I'll never forgive you."

Nugget of News: Whenever they were in New York, they stayed with us. No dis to Tom and Mika, but they were back and forth to Phoenix often, and for Tom, all over the globe when he was calling tennis matches. Though, I didn't quite understand why they didn't stay with Jamie, however, I figured it had a lot to do with Chloe wishing to keep tabs on how Hale was doing after he'd opened that box.

Not to mention, Chloe adored that room. It was modern and spacious and had an insane view.

But my stomach bottomed out when she said that.

I wasn't sure I'd regain use of it when Hale chuckled and called in return, "That's not ever going to be a problem."

Suddenly feeling numb with panic, I vaguely noticed the weird look Chloe shot him before Judge pulled her into their room, calling his goodnights, and Hale, his hand to the small of my back, guided me into ours.

He closed the door behind us and went directly to the walk-in closet.

I stood immobile, thinking mention of a nursery was the perfect segue.

Just put it out there. It wasn't your fault, it wasn't his. It happens. It's life. It's actually a miracle. And you both need to deal and then plan.

Even after giving myself this mental pep talk, the reason I slowly became unstuck and followed Hale to the closet, and once there, I simply started to disrobe and didn't say word one about my pregnancy, was twofold.

One, that night he got news his father did something beautiful and kind (again), and I needed to give him space to deal with it.

Sure, he seemed okay about it.

But it was important to be sure he was okay before laying another big, emotional issue on him.

Two, if he felt anything other than what I felt—elated that we made a baby together, no matter if it was unexpected (and truthfully, in our relationship, too soon)—I knew myself. I knew I'd never forget that reaction. I knew it'd fester inside me. It might even change the way I felt about him.

We would bounce back. Our love was strong. Fierce. I believed in us.

But it would always be there.

That said, I knew he didn't want children, so I also knew that could happen.

Wait.

No.

The reasons I started getting ready for bed without broaching the topic was threefold.

The last one being I was chickenshit.

"You okay?"

Hale's question made me jump and turn to him, hoping I was hiding I was doing it guiltily, and knowing I failed when I saw his brows draw together at witnessing my body starting.

"I'm fine," I told him, and it wasn't a lie...as such.

"Do you still have that headache?" he asked.

"No, it's gone."

"You don't get headaches very often," he noted.

"No," I agreed.

"Something stressing you out?" he pressed.

Yes!

I shook my head, and still wearing my slacks, but having stripped off my blouse so I was only wearing a bra up top, I moved from my side of the closet to his.

I got close and put my hand to his bare chest (he was similarly attired to me, only jeans, it looked good on him, it also felt good).

I looked up into his beautiful green eyes.

Tell him, tell him, tell him! JUST TELL HIM!

That was what was screaming in my head.

What came out of my mouth was, "I'm just thinking about what might be going down with Tom and Mika."

The disquiet faded from Hale's face, his lips tipped up, and he curled his hand around mine and brought my fingers to his mouth for a quick kiss.

He didn't let them go, but flattened my hand back on his chest and said, "Mika is about creativity and passion and art and bohemia and being herself, not giving a fuck what anyone thinks about her. Tom hides it well,"—that brought a full smile to his mouth—"but he's conservative and traditional. He'll want his ring on her finger and the wedding certificate signed and sealed, declaring her his as pertains to the laws of the land. They've been living together for a while now. This is totally about them announcing their engagement."

Still retaining hold of my hand, he slid his other arm around me and kept talking.

"It seems spontaneous, and I'm sure Mika can be spontaneous, but Tom really can't. Kayla got a call weeks ago from him asking about your and my schedule for this weekend and requesting she make sure she didn't schedule anything for Saturday afternoon or evening. I'm sure he, or Teddy, did the same with everyone else."

Teddy, by the by, was Mika's PA.

Hale wasn't done sharing. "It was supposed to be a surprise, but Kayla let it slip when Javi and I were going over our calendars for the next couple of months."

I temporarily lost my guilt at being a wuss in order to be miffed.

I mean, I *was* a celebrity journalist.

It was my job to know all.

"And you didn't tell me?" I demanded.

He grinned. "Baby, that would spoil the surprise for you."

"Oh," I mumbled.

"Yeah," he replied.

I liked surprises, and Hale knew it.

Like when he whisked me away to Turks and Caicos for a long weekend.

That was a great surprise.

Or when I came home to a Chopard box on the kitchen counter, and I saw he bought me a floating diamond watch he'd seen somehow "in passing" (how "in passing" it could be, I didn't know, since Hale was allergic to shopping), and he knew right away I had to have it (and he was very correct, that watch was so gorgeous, I *had to have it* even before I knew it existed).

The watch would be a longer-lasting great surprise, but the memories we made on Turks and Caicos would be forever.

And not only because we made a baby there.

Hale took me out of my thoughts by kissing my nose.

When he lifted up, he gave me a squeeze with both arm and hand.

"Stop worrying," he urged. "It's all good. Though, I would buy a new outfit if I were you. It might be a surprise, but it's still going to be a party."

It seemed a waste to buy a new outfit when, in two or three months, I'd start growing out of it.

But now that I'd backed myself into this particular corner, I couldn't get out.

"It's good Chloe's in town then. More bonding time with your sister," I noted.

"Perfect," Hale veritably purred, so content was he that Tom and Mika were (more than likely) engaged, his family was all coming to the city, I got along with his sister (she hadn't been sure about me in the beginning, but I won her over), and life was good.

I felt that purr twine warm around my heart at the same time snake sickeningly through my belly, a contrast of emotion that felt strange, and not in a good way.

Even if that purr said lovely things about where Hale was in that moment, I had to ask what I asked next. It was my job as his partner.

More, it was my blessing as the woman who loved him, who he loved in return.

Even so, I'd learned to tread softly.

"Are you okay about Chloe and Judge's diamonds?" I whispered.

I got another squeeze and a, "Yeah."

He made to let go of me, but I held on.

"Hale," I warned.

"Baby..."

He sighed, shook his head.

Then he carried on, "It's like he's still here. It's like he's a part of us. It's like he's celebrating the moments in our lives that are important to celebrate."

When he stopped talking, I nodded and encouraged him to continue, saying, "Yes?"

"And it's a reminder he wasn't sitting in the front row with Genny and Tom and you and Mika, where Chloe would put him, make no mistake, when she and Judge got married. It's a reminder of all he's missing."

"It's a reminder of how much you all miss him," I said gently.

He gave a soft grunt, which was an affirmation.

"Do you wish these things would stop?" I asked.

"And have him be really gone?" he asked in return. At my nod, he stated, "Fuck no."

"It's just hard," I surmised.

"I sometimes think, 'He gets to do the talking, but I'd give everything if I could just have one more conversation with him.' But I don't get that, and I never will."

Oh, my beautiful Hale.

I pulled my hand from his so I could curve both arms around him.

He let me hold him, and later, after Hale made love to me, and I could hear his even breathing as he spooned my back, the warmth around my heart started dissipating as that snake coiled in my gut, clearly ready to stay for a while.

Because I should have told him.

Regardless that his father had come back into his life in the only way he could, and that was a hit, no matter how velvet, it would have given him the chance of dealing with it all at once.

I was lying in the bed I'd made myself of guilt and cowardice when the lightbulb lit.

Genny.

Genny was coming to town.

She wasn't Hale's birth mom, but there was no arguing she was his true mom. She knew him better than anybody, save Tom (and now me).

I could tell her. And she could advise how to tell him.

And maybe do some divination and share how she thought he'd react.

A path out of the dark forest I'd put myself in coming clear, I finally closed my eyes, and snug in the curve of my love's long body, it took some time, seeing as that snake got comfortable.

But eventually, I fell asleep.

CHAPTER 3

GET REAL

Elsa

*B*ecause Hale wasn't into that kind of thing, and neither was I, the world at large (in other words, the media) never got the official confirmation from "our people" that he and I were getting married.

However, it wasn't lost on anybody I was living with him both in NYC and LA.

Not to mention, I had a huge, gorgeous rock on my left finger.

I'd been gaining fame on my own merits before I met Hale, and that would have continued even if I hadn't met him.

However, needless to say, being engaged to the richest man in the world, the one who also happened to be tall, fit, young, unbelievably handsome and undeniably a good guy made my celebrity hit the stratosphere the minute the first picture of us came out post-engagement. A picture that featured a little square box to the side of the one of the two of us together, that box a blown-up shot of my hand and ring.

So, the day after we got our texts from Tom, and I did some emergency texting of my own, as I wended my way through an upscale restaurant that was only three-quarters full due to the hour (that being three in the afternoon) toward Imogen Swan, America's Sweetheart, even the cynical, snobbish, well-to-do of New York couldn't hide their interest.

Many sets of eyes followed me.

Fortunately, as with everything, you got used to it.

And with this, I did what Hale did.

I ignored it.

Genny was in a corner back booth, and she slid out of it when I made the table.

We touched cheek to cheek, both sides, before she slid back in, and I took the chair opposite her.

She began our discussion by begging, "Please tell me this urgent meeting is about the fact you're ready to start planning your wedding. I never thought I'd say this after Chloe's extravaganza and all the moving parts that nearly did both our heads in. But in retrospect, I have to admit, it was really fun. The party was even more fun. And with Sasha firmly engaged in finding herself, and not even dating, right now, you're my only hope."

Oh boy.

Although I was excited she was excited to help me plan my wedding (Genny and I had a bumpy start too, though I'd won her over in less than an hour), this wasn't a good start to our current conversation.

Hale and I got engaged early, just months into our relationship.

We'd then made a pact not to start planning the wedding for a year so we had more time to settle in, not only to our relationship, but to the big changes happening in both our jobs that included having homes and offices on two different coasts.

It'd taken us two months just to figure out what to do with Cheddar and Frosty when we were in LA (after consultations with three different vets, all of which Hale patiently attended with me (even if they all three said the same thing), it was decided, since he had a personal jet, they'd go with us, and fortunately, with us being their touchstones, they didn't show any stress at doing this).

I hadn't even broached the wedding with him, and not just because we had over half a year to go before we could dig into plans.

No.

It was because I already knew what I wanted—*precisely* what I wanted—so when it came down to the actual planning, it was going to be a piece of cake.

Now, it'd have to wait even longer, because my vision for my gown did not go with a baby bump.

"No," I answered Genny. "We're still a few months out on that."

She fake pouted her disappointment, and then I saw it hit her that I'd asked for this urgent meeting, just her and me, and it wasn't about something joyous, like planning a wedding.

It was about something joyous, just not planning a wedding.

However she didn't know what that joyous thing was.

"Is everything all right?" she asked carefully, watching me closely.

"I have something important to talk to you about."

"Does this something important involve Hale?"

"Yes," I confirmed.

"And diamonds?" she went on.

Diamonds?

Oh.

Chloe and Judge's wedding bands.

I shook my head.

"I can verify, as you'd expect, it was a hit," I informed her.

I then went forth delicately, because the hits Hale kept getting from his dad were the same Genny was getting, considering Corey was her best friend.

"But we talked about it and he told me it felt like his dad was around for the important stuff, even if he isn't around. Obviously, that part feels good to him. It's just frustrating that his father gets all the say, and Hale can't share important things he has to share."

"Corey wasn't one to let many get a word in anyway," she replied.

This didn't come as a surprise. Even though I hadn't met him, Hale's dad still made it clear he'd indisputably had a forceful personality.

"I know this hurts you as much as it hurts Hale," I said quietly.

She smiled a small smile, but I was pleased to see it wasn't sad, then explained her smile.

"Elsa, honey, there is no bad part for me of Corey showing my daughter how much he loved her and how happy he would be she found a good man and a forever love by giving her diamonds." She flipped out a hand. "In the beginning, as all Corey had set up before he left us unfolded, it was bittersweet. Now, I think about how much work it was, how thorough it was, what all of it says about what we meant to him, and it's just sweet." She tipped her head to the side. "Overwhelming, as Corey could also be with his generosity, but sweet."

"I hope Hale gets there," I murmured.

"He will." She reached out and touched her mother's engagement ring that was on my finger. A ring Marilyn Swan gave Corey to give to Hale so he could give it to the woman he wanted to spend the rest of his life with. That woman turning out to be me. "I think he already is feeling more of the sweet."

God, I hoped so.

The waiter came, and I ordered a sparkling water.

Genny had a glass of rosé in front of her.

"Do you have to go back to work after this?" she asked after my non-alcoholic beverage order once the server left.

"Yes, just for a bit," I answered.

"Ah," she said, picking up her glass.

"That, and I'm pregnant."

Her body jolted, she choked on wine and had quick enough reflexes to do her spit-take into the napkin she raised to her mouth.

It would have been funny, but obviously, considering the circumstances, it was not.

"I'm sorry?" she asked after she'd wiped her mouth and put her wineglass back down.

"That's the urgency. I'm pregnant. And you saw the interview I did with Hale."

"Yes," she said.

"So you saw him declare he didn't want children."

She seemed confused. "I don't remember him saying that during the interview."

"Considering he said he never intended to find a partner, it was implied. But he *has* said that to me privately."

"Honey, as you just reminded me, I'll remind you he also said he didn't want to get married and what? Six months? Seven? Whatever it was, you had his ring on your finger."

"Last night, Chloe threatened she'd never forgive us if we turned her bedroom into a nursery, and Hale told her that she never had to worry about that."

Her expression changed completely, and troublingly, and she murmured, "Oh dear."

Oh dear wasn't the half of it.

"You can say that again, about a thousand times."

"Was he joking?" she asked.

"No. At least I don't think so."

"I take it you haven't told him about the baby."

"No!"

Genny jumped because this unexpectedly came out as nearly a shout.

But I'd been in a slow burn freakout since the news was confirmed, and now that I was talking about it, that burn was flaring out of control.

But Genny's eyes didn't flick to the restaurant to see if people were turning to look at us.

She was focused on me as she reached out and grabbed my hand.

"Calm down, Elsa," she said gently. "It's going to be okay."

It would.

I knew it would.

At least I hoped it would.

But how hairy was the journey going to be to get there?

And how hard was that journey going to be on Hale?

"It's good. It's fine. We're going to weather this. I know it," I babbled. "It's just…what if I tell him and he's upset about it, Genny? That's quite a life change if he really doesn't want kids."

"Life changes in a variety of ways we don't expect. Hale knows that."

"This is a big one," I pointed out the obvious. "Not like we crashed our car and we had to go out and buy a new one, which is also a big one. This is the kind of change to your life that lasts *the rest of your life.*"

Her expression became shrewd. "This is a big change for you too. Are *you* okay with it?"

"My genes are recessive, his genes are dominant. This means there's a very good possibility I'll have a tall, beautiful boy or girl with thick, luscious hair and the most beautiful green eyes on the planet. And my man's rich as Croesus, so I can spoil them rotten, though, not in an obnoxious way, obviously. So, of course I'm good."

Genny's lips twitched.

"I don't want him to be disappointed, Genny," I whispered despondently.

Genny's humor fled.

Oh yes.

She understood me.

The server put my sparkling water in front of me.

"Something came up, and we need to leave earlier than expected. I'm so sorry, but can you bring the bill?" Genny requested of him.

"Of course," he replied before he glided away.

"What came up?" I asked Genny, who was now touching the screen on her phone.

She gave me the one-minute finger as she put her phone to her ear.

"Yes, hi, Mika. Are you busy?" Pause and then, "You're at Nora's?" Pause. "That's actually perfect. Can Elsa and I crash your party? It's important, or I wouldn't ask."

I felt my eyes grow big.

What was she doing?

"Fabulous," she said into her phone. "We're out for a drink. We need to pay the bill and we should be there, I don't know, in around twenty minutes." Pause and then, "Marvelous. See you then."

She hit the screen on her phone to disconnect the call then dropped it in her large, but understated, vintage khaki-green Lowe tote.

She did this while I asked the pertinent question. "What are you doing?"

She picked up her glass of wine and stated, "Your mother is lovely."

I sensed this was akin to southerners saying, "Ah, your mother. *Bless*," which was very much the response my mother elicited often, even from me. One of the reasons why I was sitting across from Genny at that very moment, and not my mom.

"But I fear she might not have taught you something essential that every woman should know," she went on.

This was highly likely.

"What's that?" I asked.

"No matter how big or small the problem, it is never the best idea to tackle it alone. And if you have wise women around you, your best option is to take advantage of their wisdom as often as you can."

"I hear you, and that's good advice," I conceded. "But I don't want everybody to know before Hale knows."

She reached out, grabbed my hand again, and on a squeeze, she said, "Trust me."

I didn't confirm I trusted her.

The server was there with our check, and Genny pulled her billfold out while he was standing at our table whereupon she paid in cash.

And before I even took a sip of my sparkling water, we were out of there.

―――――

Nora Ellington, of the Manhattan Ellingtons, was old money.

Old, *serious* money.

Hobnobbing with the rich and famous, as I'd been doing since Hale entered my life, I noticed the stereotype was true.

New money rubbed it in your face. Logos abounding. Gold and jewels dripping. Range Rovers pimped to the max.

Old money was like Genny's tote. It was pretty. It was stylish. It was also utilitarian. And if you didn't know what the four L's forming a square embossed in one corner meant, you might think you could get it at Target.

The living room of Nora's sprawling Central Park West apartment, a home I'd never been to (until now), was just like that.

It was gorgeous, and elegant, the value of the real estate could buy a small island, but even so, there was nothing to prove.

White walls. Soft gray furniture with lovely curves and dark wood legs. A round coffee table in the middle that looked art deco, as in, antique, crafted a hundred years ago and painstakingly cared for all that time. An understated chandelier hanging over all of this, an even more understated rug in severely muted tones of yellow, blue, green and peach under it (a rug that was probably made of silk). Pots of healthy plants. Vases of unassuming flowers. Lovely art on the walls. And zero knickknacks on surfaces.

The only extravagance was a black grand piano in the back corner by the window, but even though Nora had three children, it wasn't covered in silver-framed, black and white, carefully posed photos. Instead, the lid was angled up.

The front door was opened by Mika, wearing a body-hugging, tan sweater dress that swept down to the ankles of her chocolate suede, high-heeled boots.

As we hit the living room, Nora swanned in wearing a pair of high-waisted, wide-leg aubergine trousers that were so long, they covered her shoes Victoria Beckham-style (though I could tell she, too, was wearing heels), and a fitted black turtleneck. No pendant dangling down her front. No bangles jangling at her wrists. Just princess-cut diamond studs in her ears.

Sure, I could tell those diamond studs were over three carats, but she probably inherited them from her mother or some great aunt.

And again, her whole vibe said she had nothing to prove.

Truth told, I wanted to be like Nora when I grew up. She was loyal. She was hilarious. She raised more money for charity than she owned, which was quite a feat, so she was thoughtful and kind-hearted.

But much like Mika, which could be a reason why they were so close, she was who she was. She said what she had to say (and one could just say she had a variety of opinions, and they were strong ones), and if you didn't like it, that was your issue, not hers. She did what she wanted to do, and the same went.

The only area in her life where I saw her holding back was with Jamie.

It had gotten to the point it was painful watching the two of them together, because it was so obvious she was in love with him. It was equally obvious she thought he'd never move on from his beloved wife who died (now, some time ago) of cancer. And again equally obvious she was not catching a single clue that he'd fallen as deep for her as she had for him, he was just ailing from a chronic case of grief mixed with denial.

"Fabulous!" Nora decreed when her gaze hit Genny and me. "An impromptu party. I'm calling down to the concierge and having them go get us a cheese soiree from Zabar's. And some truffle mouse pâté." She thought about it and concluded, "And, obviously, caviar."

Genny didn't lead into it gently.

She immediately declared, "Elsa can't have pâté. Or caviar."

Mika and Nora stood perfectly still and stared at me.

Then Mika let out an excited cry and I was in her arms.

"Oh, Elz, I'm so pleased for you," she said into my ear, all her obvious pleasure gliding over my skin, pleasure about something I was pleased about too. It started soaking in, and instead of doing what it should have been doing, it woke up that snake in my belly so it started writhing, which of course had me bursting into tears.

I was on a soft-gray couch with three mothers mothering me, a wad of tissue in my hand, a tall, slender glass of ice water on a marble coaster on the table beside me, a hand rubbing my back and concerned faces all around when I finally got my shit together.

Which, sad to say, took some time.

Yeah, I'd been ruminating in cruddy headspace all day.

"Hale doesn't want children," Genny explained when I was dabbing my eyes and down to sniffles.

"Ah," Nora said.

"He doesn't?" Mika asked, now openly shocked.

"N-no," I confirmed, still sniffling.

"So, this wasn't planned," Mika said quietly.

"N-no," I repeated. "I've slotted a new show into my next streaming schedule that will be an hour-long PSA about how no birth control is one hundred percent reliable."

The ladies took seats, Genny sitting next to me on the couch, holding my hand, Nora and Mika dragging the armchairs closer so we'd have an intimate huddle.

"I don't know how to tell him," I blurted.

"'Darling, I'm pregnant' springs to mind," Nora drawled.

"Nora!" Mika snapped.

She turned her head to Mika. "Am I wrong?"

"Not exactly, but they've only been together a year and this is hardly a minor blip," Mika returned.

"Not even a year," I put in. "We had our first date and then he disappeared from my life for months."

Mika threw a hand out to me, but her gaze was still on Nora. "See? So this has to be finessed."

"Although our Elsa is quite clever, I don't believe anyone can *finesse* a pregnancy," Nora retorted.

I turned to Genny, because if this was womanly wisdom, I was out.

Genny gave me an exposed clenched teeth look before she said, "I kinda agree with Nora."

"How against having children is he?" Mika asked.

"Well, he mentioned it and both his parents weren't the greatest." I looked to Genny and added hurriedly, "Even if Corey tried." I turned back to the other two. "So I can see why it's not something he wants. And just last night, he told Chloe our guest room was never going to be turned into a nursery."

"Has he, per chance, spoken to you about what *you* want in terms of family planning?" Nora asked.

Holy shit.

I could tell those two words exploded from my face by the way all three women sighed and sat back.

This time, Genny took the lead.

"It can be very easy, especially for women, to fall into the trap of tying themselves in knots to cushion every blow their man, then their children, might experience. And it's a beautiful response to have, wanting to protect the ones you love. In your instance, you learned that behavior early. Hale hadn't processed his father's suicide. Instead, he threw himself into work, and buried it. You got caught in it surfacing. And now, maybe, you're caught in a habit of trying to cushion his blows."

Some of this was not quite true.

Actually, I was the reason it surfaced. Falling for me forced Hale out of the cocoon he'd built around himself to keep out emotion he didn't want to feel and memories he'd long buried.

Though the part about being caught in cushioning Hale from life definitely was true.

"I'm absolutely not saying you should deny yourself that protective instinct," Genny went on. "What I'm saying is, don't lose yourself to it."

"Do you want children?" Mika asked.

I nodded.

"Have you always wanted children?" she inquired.

I nodded and added, "Even more so now that I know they'll be Hale's."

"And that, my dearest, is how you tell him," Nora decreed.

"I worry that he's going to be upset," I noted.

"It's hardly anyone's fault," Mika stated.

"I know that, and he'll know it. But if he's upset..."—I resisted the near overwhelming urge to put my hand on my stomach—"I'm only two months in, but it's already ours. And I'm...it's...it's suddenly *everything*. And if he doesn't feel the same way..." I didn't finish that thought.

"Then he doesn't," Nora said. "But he loves you and he'll get with the program."

"It'll always be there," I said.

"Darling," Nora started quietly, leaning so far my way, she put her elbows on her knees, "listen to Mother."

I loved it when she referred to herself as "Mother." It was hilarious.

But now I was listening to her so hard, it was like she actually was my mother.

"He might forget your birthday," she stated. "Your anniversary. To send flowers when you're nominated for an Emmy."

That made me smile.

Nora smiled back and continued, "What I'm saying is, they all seem perfect at first, but they're not, and that's not a bad thing. No one is perfect, Elsa. It's time. Take Hale off the pedestal you've put him on and get real about your lives together."

Get real about your lives together.

Okay, yes.

Turns out Genny was right.

Womanly wisdom was the shit.

"One more thing," Genny put in, and I looked to her. "I know you know, everyone in this room knows, that Hale loves you deeply, and even if this is a surprise, and perhaps not what he thought he wanted in his life, he's still going to love you and the baby you made together with all his heart. So let's get real about something else, honey. That being what triggered this panic when you know everything I just said is the truth."

Well...*damn.*

That was laying it out there.

And, oh yeah.

Womanly wisdom was the shit.

"The last time something big happened..." I trailed off.

Genny filled in the rest. "He broke up with you."

I closed my eyes tight, remembering that day, and the four days after it, when I thought he was lost to me forever.

Officially known as the worst four days of my life.

Genny squeezed my hand, and I opened my eyes.

"He's not going to break up with you," she assured. "And I have to apologize, because I was so involved in what Hale was feeling, what he unearthed in that box, I didn't take a second to think what you were going through and how that might stay with you."

"I think we're all guilty of that," Mika said.

"There's nothing to feel guilty for," I asserted. "Tom, Genny and Duncan's intervention in that brought him back to me."

"Yes, it worked out," Mika agreed. "But you'd just been cornered in a bathroom and slashed by Hale's stalker. Then he let his protective instinct override his rationality and we were all so focused on what was happening with Hale, we didn't look after you."

"We really dropped the ball on that one," Nora mumbled.

"Seriously, my family took care of me," I reminded them. "And you all took care of Hale. As it should be."

I turned my attention back to Genny when she squeezed my hand again.

"What we're trying to say is, you're a part of our family now, Elz. And we won't let that happen again."

That meant...

Everything.

"Oh my God!" I exclaimed irritably. "I'm going to cry again. And I'm not a crier!"

"Get used to that," Nora advised. "I wept through all three of my pregnancies."

"Chloe, cravings. Matt, temper tantrums. Sasha, tears," Genny cast her lot.

"I don't think I ate anything other than ice cream the entire time I was pregnant with Cadence," Mika put in. "After I had her, I couldn't face ice cream for years."

"I hope you got over that," Genny teased.

Mika grinned. "Cured on a visit to Italy when confronted with my first gelato stand."

Genny grinned back. "That'd do it."

"Ladies," I cut in.

Everyone looked at me.

Finding the right words was a huge part of my job.

But sitting there with these women, receiving all they were giving to me, I was at a loss.

The only thing I could think to say was what I said.

"I'm the luckiest girl in the world."

"Now, *I'm* going to cry," Genny muttered, her voice sounding hoarse.

I hugged her, and then somehow, we were all up and everybody was hugging.

I was all about the sisterhood, and I had close friends, but I wasn't a girl-huddle type of woman.

But that moment was one of the most precious of my life.

And it always would be.

CHAPTER 4

BUTTERFLIES

Elsa

Since I got sidetracked with Genny and the gang, but I had some work to get done before I could head home for the weekend, when I was finally finished, I was late getting home.

Therefore, when I walked off the elevator, Hale was moving my way.

I tipped my head for his kiss, no longer feeling panicked, but instead feeling nervous and maybe a bit excited.

Yep.

The snake had dissolved into butterflies.

"Good day?" Hale asked when he lifted his mouth from mine.

"Yes, you?"

"Glad it's the weekend."

"Me too," I replied.

Neither of us had the kind of jobs where weekends could actually be two days of rest. But we'd made a pact to do our best to keep them as clear as we could so we had time for our friends, our families, our cats, our pastimes and each other.

This one was entirely clear, and now I was seeing how Tom

managed to pull it off, because I had no doubt he got to my assistant too, or Kayla did in his stead.

"Drink?" Hale asked as he let me go.

I was about to answer by saying he should refresh his and we needed to have a chat, but since he'd started moving away, my sight-line opened up, and I saw our twelve-seater dining room table.

It was covered in shopping bags.

Chloe and Judge were at Jamie's house that night, having dinner with Jamie and Judge's sister Dru. Hale and I were set to meet Duncan and Genny for a drink later, after Sasha and Matt, the last to hit the city due to their schedules, arrived. Hale and I were going to pick them up.

But, when it came to Chloe, even though she wasn't there, her essence remained.

"Whoa," I said, moving into the space, dumping my stuff and shrugging off my coat. That accomplished, Frosty was at my ankles, and therefore it was a moral imperative to pick him up for a cuddle. This, I did before I remarked, "You weren't wrong about Chloe shopping."

"That isn't Chloe's. Her bags are up in their room," Hale said. "That's all for you."

I blinked at the bags.

Then I blinked at my man where he was in the kitchen holding a bottle of wine up and tilting it side to side in question.

I didn't answer his question.

I asked my own.

"Chloe bought all that for me?"

"No," Hale answered, putting the bottle of wine down on the counter in front of him. "Chloe shook down every designer she knows in order for them to give you shit you can wear on your shows, or when we're out, so when someone shoves a microphone in your face, you can say, 'I'm wearing Joe Shmoe.' That's what all that shit is."

I started laughing as Frosty and I walked to the kitchen and stopped on the other side of the island from Hale.

"I'm pretty sure there's no designer named Joe Shmoe," I noted.

Since I was still smiling, Hale smiled back.

I kept speaking.

"And as a stylist, what Chloe does isn't referred to as 'shaking down" designers. She's convincing them of the merits of the marketing opportunities she's offering them."

"Right," he said, still smiling.

"However, she isn't my stylist. I've been meaning to talk to her about that, because I could use—"

"Sweetheart," he cut me off. "She is now. Chloe doesn't wait for opportunities to arise, she doesn't wait to be asked, she also doesn't pitch. She bulldozes. This morning, you woke up without a stylist. You came home having one. But just so you know, that"—he jerked his chin to the coffee table—"wasn't all in a day's work. You didn't know it, but it's obvious she's been your stylist for months now."

I burst out laughing.

Seriously, I was totally falling in love with Chloe.

Frosty wriggled to get down (he loved his Mommy, but when he was done, he was done) just as Cheddar jumped up on the island.

I set Frosty on his feet while Hale stretched a hand out and Cheddar came right to him.

Watching this, my smile turned upside down.

At this juncture, Hale opened a drawer, and all humor fled as he pulled out Cheddar's treats and started feeding them to him, Cheddar taking them direct from Hale's fingers.

Yes…

While the cat was on the counter.

"Um…love of my life," I began.

Hale looked to me as he gave Cheddar another treat.

I could see his eyes dancing, and I knew he knew, but he played dumb and asked, "What?"

"Have we not had this conversation…" I inserted a meaningful and dramatic pause before I finished, "…about three dozen times?"

"Elz, as I've told you, and you've seen me do it repeatedly, I wipe down the counters before I cook."

"I don't care," I retorted. "Cats shouldn't be on counters. He has thousands of square feet to roam, *on two coasts*, and only one small area that isn't his domain. He can hack it. Frosty does."

"Frosty has a strict mom, Cheddar has a chill dad," Hale noted, giving another treat to our cat.

"Hale," I warned.

"Baby," he replied, setting aside the treats and now stroking our cat, again…*on the counter.*

"Hale!" I snapped.

"Sweetheart," he returned.

I glared.

Then I froze solid when he said, "Don't worry, beautiful. When you have my baby, the one you're carrying right now, I won't make you be the bitchy mom so I can be the kickass dad. We'll share the boss duties when the time comes. Though, fair warning, I'm still gonna go out of my way to be the kickass dad. Even so, or especially because of that, I need to get my chill on with our fur babies."

I couldn't move, however, by some miracle I forced my lips to.

"You know?"

He was watching me, and doing it closely, but I couldn't read what he was thinking.

"I kinda keep close tabs on your periods," he stated. "I'd like to say it's because I'm fine-tuned to you, which I am, but on that particular front, mostly it's about the fact you don't like to fuck when you're bleeding, and I love to fuck you, so that's not either of our favorite times of the month. And you haven't had a cycle in a while."

After he said that, he slid the wine bottle toward me to share silently that not only had my body given it away, I had.

"Though, I couldn't be sure," he said. "Last night, you confirmed it."

"Are you angry?"

His head jerked. "Am I what?"

"Angry," I whispered.

His brows drew down. "Why would I be angry?"

"You don't want kids."

"I don't?"

"You do?"

"With you?"

"Yes," I breathed.

"Yes," he stated firmly.

Yes.

He'd said *Yes*!

Firmly.

Fuck!

I was going to cry again.

"You thought I'd be mad?" he asked.

"You told me you didn't want kids."

"I said a lot of things when I was being an idiot," he pointed out. "Is that why you didn't tell me right away? You thought I'd be mad?"

"You told Chloe last night that her room would never be the nursery."

"Of course it won't be the nursery. It's all the way across the apartment from our room. The nursery is going to be next door."

Those butterflies were fluttering so much, it felt like they were going to explode and take me with them.

"Oh my God," I whispered.

"I thought you weren't telling me because you weren't happy we got pregnant," he noted.

"Why wouldn't I be happy?"

"Oh, I don't know," he said. "Your career is just taking off, and you kind of ride the far edge of ambition. We aren't married yet and haven't begun to plan our wedding. We haven't had a lot of time together, just you and me."

"Are those reasons why you might not be happy?"

"Who says I'm not happy?"

"Are you happy?"

"That you're having my kid?"

Was this conversation amazing, or annoying? I couldn't tell.

"Yes, Hale," I said with as much patience as I could muster. "That I'm having our child."

"The only problem I have with it is that Dad didn't know how to be a father, but I know, working with you and me, he'd have been a great grandfather, and our kid is never going to know how great of a grandfather he actually has."

Oh God.

It started happening again, the tears falling, this time silently.

"Baby," he whispered, watching them trace down my face.

"So you're happy," I said in a husky voice, just to make sure.

"Happy isn't the word for it," he replied "There isn't a word big enough for it, Elsa. I love you. I love kids. I love that our lives are going to be fuller and richer with having our own. I love that we get to give that to our families." He cocked his head to the side and asked, "Are you happy?"

"I'm so happy I think I'm about to burst, literally in the literal sense of that word. I have butterflies in my belly, and they're going berserk."

"You got something else in there too."

I sure did.

And my man was happy she (or he) was there.

More tears fell.

"Why are you all the way over there?" I asked.

"Because if I get near you right now, I might crush you with the hug I want to give you, and we can't have that."

God, I loved him.

More tears fell as we stared at each other.

Hale broke the silence, and he did it to say gently, "Don't ever be afraid of telling me something, baby. No matter if you think I might get mad. And never go through anything alone. It's what I give you, having someone to go through shit with. Don't do that to yourself, and don't take that honor from me."

Oh my God!

If you'd asked me one minute ago if I could love him more, I'd say it was impossible.

But the impossible just happened in a huge way.

"I have to admit, I was so worried you'd be upset, I asked Genny how to handle it," I confessed. "That's why I'm late tonight, not work. I went to meet Genny."

He didn't get angry about that either.

He nodded and murmured, "Understandable."

I had more to share, so I did that.

"She corralled Mika and Nora into a Wise Woman Session so they know too. But I've sworn them to secrecy, and Nora made up some cocktail on the spot to cement their Wise Woman Promise to me they'd keep their mouths shut, and they drank to it. I think in Nora, Genny and Mika terms that's akin to a hand on a bible in front of a judge, so we're good until we're ready to share widely. I didn't imbibe in the cocktail, for obvious reasons, but I'm looking forward to tasting it about a year from now."

"A year?"

"I'm going to breastfeed."

"Ah," he murmured. "So?" he prompted.

I gave him what he didn't exactly ask for but I knew he'd still asked for it.

"I'm two months. It happened on Turks and Caicos. March baby. Apparently, you're supposed to abstain during fertile times, which is clearly something I blocked out when I read the prescription pamphlet. You figured it out, but I was going to tell you tonight. Having a surprise new stylist averted my path, but you need to know, I was going to tell you. And we have a doctor's appointment next week for follow up and some pregnancy insight, and my obstetrician and I would like you to be there."

"I wouldn't be anywhere else."

How did I ever doubt?

"I love you madly," I whispered.

"That's good, since you aren't getting rid of me now," he quipped.

I was *so* done with this island between us, therefore I walked around.

I was barely within reaching distance when Hale reached, and he hadn't lied. When his arms closed around me, they did it so tightly, I couldn't breathe, and I feared maybe a rib or two might crack.

I didn't care.

But he was Hale, and he kinda liked me, so he didn't squeeze me and our unborn child to death. He loosened his hold but didn't let go even if he did move one hand so he could cup my jaw.

"Are you sure, sweetheart?" he queried. "This is gonna be a lot harder on you than it is on me."

"I love her, or him, almost as much as I love you."

His eyes warmed and he murmured, "Okay."

"Are *you* sure?" I asked.

"I want a her, blonde hair, blue eyes."

"I'm not sure I can make that happen."

Left unsaid: I wanted the opposite.

"Then we'll have to make another one."

And there it happened again.

I loved him more.

"How many do you want?" I asked.

"As many as you want."

I started laughing. "What if that's fifteen?"

"Okay, I'm capping it now at four."

I continued laughing.

Then I shoved my face in his chest because the emotion of this moment, the importance of it swept over me, and I was going to start crying again.

He slid his hand from my jaw up into the back of my hair.

"Hormones," I mumbled into his chest.

"Sure," he said, knowing I was lying. Then he asked, "Do you want to get married sooner?"

I tipped my head back. "Do you?"

"Sweetheart, I'm not going anywhere."

"Me either. And I want a big thing, so first, we need to pay attention to the current big thing before we get stuck into the next big thing, and second, I want the next big thing to be *big*, so don't give away all your money."

"Like I'm the only one who's loaded in our family."

Our family.

I hadn't noticed it, but the butterflies were gone. Somewhere along the line of this conversation, the exhilaration and beauty of them soaked into my flesh and became a part of me, a part of this, a part of starting a family with Hale.

"Are you going to try to one-up Chloe on the wedding gig?" he asked.

"I'm not thinking full choir like she had, but I do want to give you food for thought since it'd be important to me, and my family, if we had a Jewish wedding."

"Of course, since I'm converting."

Again, I was blinking.

"Sorry?" I asked.

"I need to talk to your rabbi," he said distractedly, like he was making a mental note.

I shook him and his focus returned to me. "Hale, are you serious?"

"I was considering it before, especially since we were going to be planning a wedding and building a family. Now things need to get moved up."

"You're going to convert," I said flatly.

His eyes narrowed on me. "Don't you want me to?"

"I just don't know how much better you can get. And it's freaking me out."

He grinned.

"But that's a big deal, Hale," I warned him.

"I know, sweetheart. But I'm not doing this just to do it. I've never been religious, but that doesn't mean I'm not spiritual. Again, I want to sit down with your rabbi, discuss what this might mean, understand it so I know I'm making the right decision. However, can I assume you want our children brought up in your faith?"

Man, suddenly there was a whole lot we needed to talk about.

I nodded.

He spoke.

"First, a family should be united in that way, even if, in the end, I find it isn't the right path for me, I still need to have the knowledge so I can help you guide our children in their faith," he declared. "Second, I've shared every high holiday with your family since we've been together, and they were meaningful to me in a number of ways, including how welcome into the community they made me feel. And, most importantly, I've always wanted to smash a glass with my foot and be hoisted up on a chair."

I started giggling, actually giggling, before the tears welled in my eyes again.

Hale stared at my eyes. "Jesus, maybe it *is* the hormones."

I batted him on the arm, but joked, "Say goodbye to Jesus."

He busted out laughing.

That fought back the tears, and I smiled at him as he did it.

His body made a sudden movement, and he quit laughing in order to focus intently on my face.

"My phone is vibrating, which means Genny and Duncan are here," he said, his words rushed.

"I thought we were meeting them later for a drink after Matt and Sasha arrived," I noted.

"Change of plans. Sidetracked by my beautiful fiancée and our future kid. We're popping out with them to have a bite before we go to the airport to meet the new arrivals. Now I need to know, and you got the time it takes the elevator to get here to answer, do you want to wait the normal three months, or are we sharing our news?"

"We're sharing, you down with that?"

"Absolutely."

"But we have to be careful not to take the wind out of Tom and Mika's sails," I warned.

"Agreed."

"Can Chloe keep a secret?"

"To the grave. Matt will be cool too. But don't tell Sasha until later. She's got a big mouth."

"Right."

"They won't mind about the conversion, although Genny and Tom are both practicing Christians. But let's leave that for later."

"Gotcha."

His face changed in a way I memorized every centimeter of it, though I didn't have to, since the vision of it was burned into my heart.

"I love you so fucking much, it hurts," he said, his voice low, but fierce.

Oh yeah.

My man was happy I was having his baby.

And I was ecstatic.

I framed his face with my hands. "Same," I whispered.

The elevator pinged.

Well, I guessed that meant we could communicate thoroughly and come to an understanding on a variety of subjects in a short period of time, because we just did it.

Hale kissed me as the doors to the elevator swished open.

I had a feeling it was supposed to be a quick peck of shared joy, but it didn't end that way.

So when we finally broke free and turned to the elevator, Duncan and Genny were standing there, Duncan's arm slung along Genny's shoulders, both of Genny's arms wrapped around Duncan's middle.

Oh, and her eyes were shining, bright and happy, and aimed at me.

"We can take a walk around the block and come back," Duncan offered.

Duncan was such a good guy.

I opened my mouth.

But Hale beat me to it.

"Elsa is having my baby."

Duncan's lips parted before they spread into a huge smile.

Genny let her husband go, clapped twice and rushed us.

I got a hug, then Hale got one while I got one from Duncan. Then Hale and Duncan did that man thing where they started with shaking hands then ended up in a one-armed hug, still clasping hands.

While they did that, Genny cupped my cheek.

"Okay?" she mouthed when I caught her gaze.

"Totally," I mouthed back.

She came in and pressed her forehead to mine.

She then moved away and turned to Hale.

"I hope you have champagne," she stated.

He didn't answer. He just went right to the wine fridge.

The cork popped and we all shouted like it was New Year's.

It was the only time in my life I was okay being around an opened bottle of champagne without a glass being offered to me.

Correction.

I wasn't just okay with it.

I was thrilled.

CHAPTER 5

PRIVATE JET

Hale

"Oh my God, how could you *even?*" Chloe demanded in a low voice, her eyes on him, and they were enraged slits.

"It was an accident," he told her, then stated firmly, "A *happy* accident."

They were sitting at the dining room table doing the first wave of breakfast.

With Elsa acting in her usual capacity as his sous chef, Hale had made scrambled eggs with goat's cheese and chives, hash browns, bacon, brioche toast, and the breakfast dessert homemade ginger nut muffins were cooling on the counter.

And he'd just shared they were pregnant.

Except for Sasha, everyone was awake, including Matt, even though, with the change in time zones, it was seriously early for him.

But Matt had always been that kind of guy, even before being pre-med turned into being pre-vet, then vet school, internship, and now he was practicing at the large animal hospital where he'd interned in Prescott.

For this visit, all Hale's siblings were staying with him, however, for the last six months, this happened every time they were in town.

Chloe and Judge should stay with Jamie, because Jamie missed his boy when he was away, not to mention he'd missed a lot of his life while he was growing up. But Hale knew Chloe put a stop to that after Hale had opened the box his dad left for him.

And Chloe wasn't the only one.

They were hovering, and he should let them off the hook, share he was okay, or more to the point, Elsa had this.

But he didn't mostly because he liked having them around.

Genny and Duncan, and Duncan's boys Sully and Gage were staying with Jamie. Alex and Rix were at Alex's dad, Ned's house.

The entire gang had gotten the text that morning reminding them the family meeting was going to be at Jamie's.

So that meant this surprise engagement party was being handled by Nora.

But that was for later.

Now, he was shocked as shit Chloe was acting like a brat.

"Babe," Judge muttered.

She whipped her head around to her husband. "No, Judge. They don't even have an *outside* so I could go out and whoop for joy in a place Sasha can't hear me. You can't just share *you're pregnant* and then tell the people you're sharing it with they have to be quiet about it because your big mouth sister is upstairs, and if we wake her by shouting and carrying on, she'll know and tell everyone so Dad and Mika's big news day will turn into Hale and Elsa's big news day."

She whipped her head back to Hale, who was now grinning.

"That was just cruel," she hissed. "*Cruel.*"

"You'll get over it," Hale replied.

"Not without a lot of pouting," she returned. "A lot," she stressed. She went back to her husband. "This means we have to get pregnant soon, darling."

Judge choked on some brioche and now his eyes were slits.

He swallowed and asked his wife, "Why?"

Chloe wafted a hand across the table. "Well, obviously all the cousins need to be close in age so they can go trick-or-treating together and have slumber parties and have a buddy when they take skiing lessons."

"Baby, we live all the way across the continent from Hale and Elsa," Judge pointed out. "That isn't conducive to trick-or-treating together."

"Not when they're in LA," she retorted.

"When they're in LA, they're six hours away, which is also not conducive to trick-or-treating," Judge shot back.

She turned her attention again to Hale. "You need to buy another plane."

"I'm not buying another plane, Coco," he returned. "Actually, I'm thinking about selling the one I have and flying commercial."

That was when Elsa choked on her brioche.

He turned his head to the side and looked at her.

She took a sip of half-caff coffee (she told him that morning her doctor wanted her off caffeine, but in order to combat the headaches she would get if she went cold turkey, the doc gave Elsa a week to titrate off the stuff) before she focused on him and declared, "I share your mission. I really want to save the planet. I really, really, really do. For you, me, everyone on the globe, and especially for our child, not to mention the children our child might have. But, handsome, you can't give a girl a private jet and then take it away."

"This is true," Chloe chimed in. "You cannot."

"I'm pretty sure all the carbon neutral stuff you're forcing on your companies means you've done your part and we get to keep our plane," Elsa went on.

"It doesn't work that way, sweetheart," he shared something he knew she knew.

"But, what will Frosty and Cheddar do?" she demanded.

"Learn to settle for first class," he replied.

She shifted her gaze to Chloe. "Seems like I need to conduct a lot more interviews."

Chloe laughed.

"Are you done?" Matt asked his sister through her amusement.

"Done with what?" Chloe asked back.

Matt didn't answer.

He got up, walked around the table, and held out his hand to Hale.

Hale pushed his chair back and took Matt's hand, whereupon he pulled Hale out of his chair and into a hug.

"Pleased for you, man," he murmured, thumping Hale's back. "Thrilled." He let Hale go, bent to kiss Elsa's cheek and said, "Really happy for both of you."

"Thanks, Matt," Elsa said quietly, smiling at him and watching as he walked back to his seat.

She hadn't gotten a lock on Matt yet, and since that was her thing, and she thought she was failing at it with Matt, it was killing her.

He'd tried to tell her Matt was a unique guy. Ridiculously smart, not exactly an introvert, but far from an extrovert. He didn't readily open up, and when he did, it was rare and solely done with a carefully curated crew that was small (and fortunately, Hale was a member). He was protective of his mother and sisters, and fiercely loyal.

Not too long ago, Matt had come out to the family as bi, but since, he'd only dated women.

Outside of that last part, Matt reminded Hale of Hale's dad, and it wasn't the first time he thought that Matt was far more like Corey than Hale was. If Matt wasn't the spitting image of Tom, there'd be uncomfortable questions, but he was, and he got that mad protective streak from his father.

Elsa was convinced there was more to it, something he was holding back, and suggested Matt was worried how his sexuality would reflect on his parents if it was known publicly. Thus, she was concerned he was burying that part of himself to protect his family.

Although Hale knew Matt had been concerned about how Tom would take it, considering Tom veered more toward the traditional, when Matt came out, Tom didn't give a fuck. And once that hurdle was passed, Hale knew the only thing holding Matt back was his acute focus on his studies, and now, building his practice.

"When the time comes, Matt will do what Matt needs to do," he'd told Elsa. "He'll find who's right for him, if that's what he wants. With Chloe being so forcefully affectionate, and Sasha so flower-child loving, they overshadow Matt, and I promise, he's good with that. He works better in the shadows left to do his own thing. He thrives there. But he has his ways of showing his love. You'll learn how he is. But, trust me, that's the way of it. So don't worry."

Now, she was studying Matt while eating and pretending not to study Matt, and Hale was thinking his woman was all kinds of cute.

On that thought, his phone started vibrating, which meant, as planned, the others were arriving, he just didn't know which others they would be. Duncan, Genny, Sully and Gage or Rix, Alex, Blake and Ned.

What he did know was it was time to scramble more eggs and fry more hash browns for the second wave.

He got up, kissed the top of Elsa's head and headed to the kitchen.

The doors to the elevator opened, expelling Duncan, Genny, Sully and Gage, but as usual, it was Gage who opened his mouth first.

"God, I'm not even two steps in and I'm salivating for whatever you're cooking," he announced at the same time he was rubbing circles on his gut.

"Do they know?" Genny asked excitedly, after ascertaining the table didn't include Sasha.

"Know what?" Sully queried.

"We know," Matt shared.

"Know what?" Gage repeated after his brother.

"You have to be quiet about it," Duncan said to his son. "You know Sash, and this is Tom and Mika's day. Sasha can learn tomorrow."

"Know what?" Sully repeated.

"Elsa and I are having a baby," Hale announced.

Sully grinned. Gage grinned bigger.

"*You're having a baby?*" Sasha shrieked from the stairs.

"Shit," Hale muttered at the same time Chloe mumbled, "*Merde.*"

Sasha had planted her hands on her hips and her eyes were locked on Duncan. "What did you mean, 'you know Sash?'"

"Honey, you're not exactly good at keeping secrets," Duncan said gently.

"I'm great at keeping secrets," she declared, or more to the point, lied through her teeth.

"Judge, darling, get the fire extinguisher. Sasha's pants are about to ignite at any second," Chloe drawled.

Sasha stormed down the steps, saying, "Okay so I let some things slip once or twice."

"You told my ex-girlfriend what I was giving her for Christmas," Gage said.

"You told Dad and Genny I was thinking of moving to New York before I even agreed to come visit the company that was trying to recruit me," Sully said.

"You told Dad it was me who used all his tennis balls to teach our dog not to be afraid of the pool," Matt said.

"You told Genny I stole all the meatballs she made for Dad and took them with me back to school," Gage kept at it.

"You told Rix I told you I thought Alex being shy was hot," Sully kept at it too. Then added, "And you told him I thought Alex was just plain hot."

"You told my roommate I ate the cookies his mom baked him after I'd convinced him some guys down the hall ate them," Matt put in.

"You told Genny and Tom I used their brand-new couch to slide into third base with my girlfriend when I was a junior in college," Hale added.

Chloe kept her mouth shut, but the brow she arched toward her sister spoke volumes.

Sasha's face was red after all this, though she didn't verbally cop to it, probably because it served no purpose. They already knew it was her, she could deny none of it.

Instead, she griped, "You all can't possibly know how it's feels to be left out of something this big when everyone else in your family knows it."

"Then my sunny, darling, beautiful girl," Genny started, "perhaps there's a lesson to be learned here."

Sasha glared at her mother then she came to Hale and gave him a sideways hug.

"Happy for you, bro," she said, then to Elsa, "You too, Elz. Terrific news."

"Thanks, Sash," Elsa replied.

Hale just put his arm around her waist, gave her a squeeze and asked quietly, "Wanna help me with the eggs?"

"Defo," she replied.

"Throw some butter in the pan, honey," he muttered.

Coffee mugs were filled. Muffins were claimed. Rix, Alex, Ned and Blake showed and got the news, and more excitement, well wishes and hugs were shared.

The table was buzzing. Another batch of eggs was in the sauté pan. Hash browns in another. And now Chloe was in the kitchen with him keeping the toast flowing, the fresh coffee brewed.

That was when he felt it.

He looked to where it was emanating from, and he saw Elsa's eyes tracking him.

When he caught them, she blew him a kiss but didn't stop watching him, an expression of sheer contentment on her gorgeous face.

Now, Elsa was an extrovert. She liked people. She liked buzz. Energy. She also had a complicated family dynamic, so she loved how close Hale's family was, for him, whereas Hale loved he could give that to her.

Thus, right then, she was in her perfect element.

But she wasn't feeling contentment for her.

Hale's family was at his table.

It was contentment for him.

Christ, he loved her.

And he was feeling that so much in that moment, the tightness that began forming in his neck last night when Elsa confirmed she was pregnant didn't register.

That said, it also didn't go away.

CHAPTER 6

THE GUESTS ARRIVED

Hale

"You slid into third base on Genny and Tom's new couch?"

They were sitting in the back of his car, Paul driving, Hudson, one of their bodyguards, sitting next to Paul in the front seat.

They were on their way to Jamie's.

Breakfast consumed, before they left, Elsa had turned her attention to marking the event in her usual manner: donning an outfit that played havoc with Hale's cock.

Today it was a long, full, pleated silk skirt in a coppery color that flirted with her legs and skimmed her ass with a long-sleeved, rust-colored sweater cropped at the waist. On her feet was a pair of bronze pumps with a lethally thin heel.

"I told you about that," he reminded her.

"Yes. You told me you told Matt, and Matt, who had, until somewhat recently, a blind spot in regards to his little sister's large mouth, told Sasha, who in turn told Tom and Genny. But you didn't say it was a *brand-new* couch," she returned. She then purred, "You're a very bad boy, Hale Wheeler."

That did things to his cock too.

But unfortunately he wasn't in a position to act on it.

Instead, he chuckled and leaned in to touch his mouth to hers.

When he pulled away, he didn't go far because she said, "I loved this morning."

"I could tell," he replied.

It was then she leaned in to touch her mouth to his.

When she was done, she settled in her seat, and he took the opportunity of Saturday NYC traffic and some alone time to touch base about important things.

"You ate okay," he noted. "Are you having morning sickness?"

She shook her head. "Not yet, thank God."

"Was it just missing your periods that sent you to the doctor?"

"That and the five positive pregnancy tests I took."

He chuckled again, then asked, "Anything else I need to know in the now?"

The love she felt for him, liberally mixed with the happiness she felt from where this unexpected turn in their lives was taking them, shone out of her face so brightly, he needed sunglasses.

It also sent tension driving into his neck.

"My doctor gave me some pamphlets that I've read. I'll let you have a look at them. But there really isn't much I need to worry about, except what you know. Avoiding some foods, definitely alcohol, most medications, except Tylenol, and getting off caffeine. I've got some vitamins I've started taking. I can exercise as normal. The rest for now is just be healthy."

As she spoke, he twisted his neck to relieve some of the pressure, and her eyes dropped to his movement.

But when she was done talking, he teased, "You exercise?"

She gave a haughty, one-shouldered shrug. "I will admit, having constant access to my own personal driver has reduced the amount of steps I take during a day. So obviously I needed to incorporate more shopping into my weekly regime to make up for it. Something, as you know, I've done."

He smirked.

She reached out and curled her fingers around his thigh. "You okay?"

"I'm great."

"If you're great, honey, then why are you rolling your neck?"

Fuck.

He wouldn't think he'd ever feel like she could know him too well.

But with that question, Hale felt she knew him too well.

He wrapped his fingers around hers on his leg and replied, "I'm fine."

"If something's troubling you—"

Hale cut her off. "Nothing's troubling me. We had a great morning. We're headed to a celebration that's been a long time coming. I was wrong, I'm not fine. Like I said, I'm great." He pulled her hand to his mouth, brushed his lips to her knuckles and looked direct in her eyes. "I'm happy, baby."

"Okay, handsome," she whispered.

She said that, but he could feel the intensity of her focus, and he felt relief when she broke it and turned to gaze out the side window, her fingers still curved tight around his.

But it was then Hale had to turn his attention to why he wasn't sharing the fact that what he'd just asserted was a half-truth.

He *was* great. He was marrying a phenomenal woman he loved to his soul. She was having his baby. His family was all close, emotionally, and at that moment, physically.

But he was also on edge. He knew it. He felt it, and not just the tightness at the base of his skull.

After what went down with him and Elsa, he'd had several conversations with Tom and Jamie about avoiding that ever happening again.

Learning to be more self-aware was key, even if it wasn't easy.

So he knew something was bugging him. The reason he didn't mention it to his woman was because he didn't know what it was.

Naturally, he couldn't talk about it unless he knew what he was talking about.

More to the point, he wanted Elsa happy. He wanted her focused on what was happening with her life, her body, how this was going to affect her career and how she'd handle that.

Above all, he didn't want her stressed. He wanted her to feel his support and know he had her back, not thinking she had to see to his needs and tie herself in knots to make life run smoothly for him.

She'd already delayed an entire day telling him they were starting a family, going so far as to seek out Genny in how to handle him, because she was worried about his reaction.

So…yeah.

That was a part of why he was struggling.

He felt shit he'd conditioned his fiancée to tread so damned lightly when it came to his feelings.

Though, he wasn't pissed about it, at least not at Elsa.

But he was pissed at himself.

Eventually, Jamie's brownstone came into view, and knowing the drill, when Paul double-parked outside, he and Elsa waited until Hudson got out and did a scan. They knew he deemed it safe when he opened Elsa's door.

She folded out, Hale exited behind her, and Hudson followed them up the steps.

The door was open before they got there and Cadence was standing in it.

She was grinning widely, but Hale felt something shift in his chest when he took her in, because Mika's girl was smart, sweet and beautiful, but she was also her mother's daughter. At her age of twenty, she was forming a definite point of view, and she had a great deal of creative ambition. This manifested itself in a documentary she'd worked with her mom to film, edit and release, to some buzz and promising critical reviews.

She'd now started blocking out her next project, which was another documentary, but this one she was going to do on her own.

In other words, she was a busy woman, and she tended to look like that, with more important things on her mind than makeup, hair and the perfect outfit.

This didn't mean she didn't have style. But it leaned toward wide-leg jeans, graphic tees, slouchy sweaters, or short skirts, tights and high-top Doc Martens.

Now she was wearing a short, wraparound dress in a wispy fabric that had an understated pattern of browns and peaches, and long, full sleeves that were blousy and sheer. With this, she wore high, strappy heels.

Growing up with Genny (then Chloe and Sasha), he had a lifetime of knowing when a woman's hair and makeup was done professionally.

Right now, Cadence's was just that.

On their way up the steps, he glanced down at Elsa to see her already looking up at him, her brows raise to communicate she was thinking the same thing he was.

And...oh yeah.

Something was up, and it wasn't the something they thought it was.

"Fantastic!" Cadence cried while giving them hugs. When she stepped back to let them inside, she said, "Now we only have to wait for Inger and Emilie, and we can get this gig started."

"What...exactly...*is* this gig?" Elsa asked while Cadence shut the door.

Cadence didn't answer.

She said, "Come in. It's cocktail hour."

He and his woman shared another glance while they moved into Jamie's living room, but they didn't have time to prod further. The room was packed, and although most the people there had been at his breakfast table, David, Elsa's father, his girlfriend, Kristine, Oskar, Elsa's brother, and Dru, Judge's sister, had not been. Therefore, they were engaged in hellos and hugs.

Noticeably absent, though, were Nora, Jamie, Mika and Tom.

Further, Hale could smell garlic and herbs.

Something was cooking, in more than one way.

Running interference for Elsa, since her dad and brother didn't know she was pregnant, Hale circumvented her cocktail and made her some sparkling water and cranberry juice in a martini glass so those who hadn't heard the news would learn it with the attention it deserved.

"Anybody know what's going on?" Hale asked as he stood with Elsa, David, Kristine and Oskar.

"No idea, but I'd like to make it official I'm at one with a command of attendance to a family meeting that involves two o'clock cocktails," David remarked before taking a sip of his.

Oskar was scowling at his phone.

"Everything cool?" Hale asked him.

Oskar shoved his phone in his back pocket, saying, "Life is lessons. And the lesson I'm learning now is my mother and baby sister tend toward being pains in the asses."

Hale understood him.

Oskar was right then on a very bumpy patch on the road of life. His divorce was recently final. He had half custody of two very young children. And for the first time as an adult, he was back at home in New York after living in Boston for years, making a family and practicing law.

His ex didn't want a divorce, which made that scenario iffy for a good while.

Along with that, he'd had to find a new job, and house, and set up the latter for himself and his children, a task in New York that was rife.

And for the first time since he left home to start his undergrad, as a full grown adult, he was experiencing the caprices of his mother and youngest sister.

Hale and Oskar didn't see eye to eye on a number of things, but after a rocky introduction, he'd been pleased to learn the man was solid. He loved his children completely. And it had been a privilege to watch as Oskar and David worked at figuring out their relationship as two grown men, before they started settling into it.

But he felt for the guy.

Because Hale knew from experience having a mother that thought the world revolved around her was not fun in the slightest, and with Inger, it included almost stifling adoration of her only son. This was something Oskar could enjoy when he lived in another state, but being close, it was overpowering.

As for Emilie, she'd had some hard knocks lately too. But instead of doing something she'd managed not to do even if she was deep in her twenties—growing up—she often acted out because the world wasn't falling in line with what she considered her worldview.

And that, particularly, drove Oskar right up the wall.

"Let me guess," Elsa drawled, "they're running late."

"Emilie says ten minutes out, which means at least twenty," Oskar told her.

Hale didn't miss David's lips going tight and Kristine's sudden interest in the corner of the room.

Yeah, they all knew the drill, and none of them liked it.

"Whatever this is, and I think we all know it's not a family meeting, can start without them," Hale declared. "My sense is, there's catering staff here, and they can open the door if we're otherwise engaged."

Oskar's eyes fell on Dru across the room, he muttered, "I'll go see to that," and he moved away.

"You look especially beautiful today," David said to Elsa, watching her like he was trying to figure something out.

This was true and not. She always looked beautiful and had impeccable style.

But for certain, the glow was discernable.

"Things have been busy with whatever this is, but we need a Cohen family meeting very soon," Elsa told him.

For a moment, David seemed nonplussed.

That moment didn't last long before his gaze flew back and forth between Hale and Elsa, his eyes lit, and then they grew moist.

Christ.

The man had guessed.

He'd *guessed* his daughter was pregnant.

That didn't give Hale any tension.

That made Hale wish all the more they were going to have a daughter so he could be as connected to her, as close and loving, as David and Elsa were.

Elsa got near to her father because she knew he'd guessed too.

"Dad, this is about Mika and Tom," she warned low.

"Are you...?" he asked.

"Yes," she confirmed.

Immediately, David handed off his cocktail to Kristine and engulfed his daughter in a hug.

Kristine shot Hale a confused look, and all he could do was tip his head to the side.

When David let his girl go, he touched her cheek and whispered, "My baby."

"Always," she replied.

Shit.

Hale's throat got tight.

Yeah, he hoped like fuck they had a daughter, either this one, or one of the three to come.

"Matt? Hale?"

He turned at Jamie calling his name and saw the man standing in the doorway.

"Could you come with me?" Jamie requested.

"Apparently, this show is getting on the road," he muttered, smiled at David and Kristine, kissed Elsa's cheek, then he and Matt walked to Jamie.

Jamie said nothing, he just led them through his house to the back, and then out to the garden.

"Holy fuck," Hale whispered as the emerged into the space, at the same time Matt murmured, "Jesus Christ."

There were rods of lights dripping from the trees, shooting ones coming out of planters and the bedding beside the flagstone decking and walkways. Also snugged among the plants in the edging and urns were flickering, battery-operated pillar candles, dozens of them.

And at the far end of the garden, an arch had been erected. It hung to the ground with fringe that at the top had some macramé, and shooting from the sides were fluffy beige fronds of some plant, these liberally mingled with greenery and cream, peach and orange flowers.

Two massive tufts of these arrangements shot from the base at each side, intermingled with more pillar candles.

It was daytime, but Jamie's back garden was shaded and filled with foliage, so it always seemed like a sheltered, shadowy sanctuary. This had been used to its fullness with the lighting and decorations.

Tom was walking toward them from the arch.

He wasn't wearing a tux. He was in a dark brown, three-piece, bespoke suit with a peach tie. His precisely tipped pocket square was orange.

Jamie faded back into the house when Tom arrived at his two sons and said, "What do you say? You boys care to stand up for your old man?"

Even as Hale's throat closed, he heard Matt's grunt.

Then they were in a group hug.

"I'll take that as a yes," Tom kidded, but his voice was gruff.

Neither Matt nor Hale had to answer.

It was a definite yes.

When they broke, Tom lifted his hands and affectionately patted both their cheeks in a way he hadn't touched Hale since he hit double digits. The nostalgic beauty of it in this moment wasn't lost on him, and he made a point to open himself up to feel its fullness.

"Honored, Dad. I hope you know. But, what's with the secrecy?" Matt asked.

"Cadence wanted a big thing," Tom explained. "Mika and I wanted to stand in front of a judge and then have a long honeymoon and a dinner party after." He grinned and continued, "Though, when we told Cadence that, she tried to hide it, but it was clear she was disappointed. We still didn't want a big thing, but we wanted something special for Cadence, and in talking about it, we realized we wanted the same for us. Mika and Nora put their heads together and..."

He lifted his arms out to his sides in conclusion.

"It's genius," Hale told him. "And beautiful."

"I had nothing to do with that part," Tom replied. "I had a suit made in the textile Mika chose and paid for stuff. This is all Mika, Cadence, Nora and Dru."

"Then it's unsurprising it's perfect," Matt said.

Tom caught his son by the back of his neck and pulled him into another hug.

When they broke, Tom fished something out of his pants pocket and offered it to Matt.

"The ceremony is going to be short because we couldn't fit everyone out here and chairs too," Tom shared. "So no need for rehearsals. Just give me that when the pastor tells you to."

It was Mika's wedding band.

"Nora and Cadence are standing up for Mika," Tom went on.

"Best reason to miss work on a Friday ever," Matt said.

"Glad you think so," Tom muttered.

"I do think so, Dad," Matt stated firmly.

In an abrupt movement, Tom straightened his shoulders.

"She's amazing," Matt continued. "We all love her. She's…" He paused, cleared his throat, but his voice was still thick when he finished, "She's perfect for you."

At that, Tom grabbed Matt's head with both of his hands and pulled it so close, their foreheads collided.

Because…yeah.

This was huge.

All of Tom and Genny's kids struggled with their divorce, but Matt struggled the most.

So, again.

Huge.

Tom kept his son close even as he let him go with one hand and yanked Hale into their knot.

"The first one was perfect too," Tom said. "I know you two know that. But this one is special, because Mika has my heart, and I'm looking forward to spending the rest of my life with her, but also because both my boys are standing up with me."

Fucking hell.

"Jesus, stop, or when they all get out here, and see the three of us blubbering like idiots, they're gonna think someone is dying," Hale joked.

They all laughed, but Tom's hold on their necks got tighter.

"God blessed me with the two best sons on the planet," he whispered.

Fuck.

Hale felt them hit his eyes. He looked to Matt and saw the same in his.

But at that point, Tom slapped them both forcefully on the shoulders, stepped back and ordered, "Suck it up, men. I told Jamie to give us ten minutes and then get the party started. It's places time."

With no need for more encouragement, Matt and Hale moved to the arch.

Tom moved to the door to the garden.

"Totally didn't see this coming," Matt said when they took their places.

"Same," Hale agreed.

"Maybe Jamie and Nora will witness this and get their heads out of their asses," Matt remarked.

"That might require an intervention," Hale replied.

"I'd take another Friday off and fly commercial to be a part of that," Matt quipped.

Hale shot him a grin.

Then, a couple of minutes later, they received their dad's second gift of the day.

Being front and center to see, and hear, the shock, amazement and delight play across faces and tumble from mouths as the guests arrived.

———

NORA WALKED OUT FIRST WEARING A SIMPLE PEACH, TO-THE-KNEE DRESS that was elegant and sensationally her. She was carrying a small poof or orange flowers in her hand.

Cadence came next, and her flowers were peach.

Finally, Mika showed, radiant in a gauzy, floor-length cream gown that had a delicate lace, off-the-shoulder bodice and long, billowy sleeves that gathered at the wrists in a ruffle. Her skirt was wide and tiered and the graceful folds moved almost ethereally as, with a bright smile and carrying a dripping bouquet of cream and peach flowers, she walked over the flagstones through the path the crowd of her loved ones had parted for her...to Tom.

When she arrived at his side, and their eyes locked, the rest of them faded away, but Hale had no qualms at being reduced to a shadow in attendance.

That said, it wasn't lost on him that the woman who had spent most of her life at Tom's side, and bore his children, was standing ten feet away.

Tom and Genny's divorce wasn't easy, but they were the kind of people who did the work to make it not as difficult as it could have been, and then some.

But this was something else.

Stealing a glance at Genny, though, he saw her standing with Duncan like they had been when he and Elsa emerged from the kiss the night before. Duncan holding his wife close, Genny having wrapped both arms around his middle. She was leaning into him heavily, Hale could see, and there were tears of happiness for Tom and Mika shimmering in her eyes.

He moved his gaze to his fiancée to see she had the same watery gaze. She felt his attention and tore hers from the happy couple to look at Hale.

She blew him a kiss.

"Love you," he mouthed.

She blew him another kiss.

He then turned his attention back to the handsome groom and his stunning bride, and he, along with the others who loved them most in this world, watched two people who deserved every happiness, receive it.

CHAPTER 7

A COCKTAIL PROMISE

Hale

"We need hazmat suits with the amount of sexual tension and unrequited lust floating around in here," Rix stated.

It was post nuptials.

It was also after they partook of a killer buffet that included an insane truffle mac and cheese that Hale was determined to copy in his own kitchen.

A wedding cake that had an artistic design of leaves and petals pressed into the smooth frosting at the sides and a tuft of the wedding décor bursting from between the two layers was set out, but had yet to be cut.

And while they were all outside, Jamie's living room, the dining room it flowed into and foyer that flowed into both had been transformed with decorations, a one-bartender bar station, small, intimate tables with centerpieces for eating at, and a variety of comfortable seating areas welcoming everyone to hang and talk.

All this was new furniture. Where Jamie's stuff went, Hale had no clue. He also had no clue how the crew managed to make such huge changes in the forty-five minutes it took to get everyone outside, have the ceremony, then pass around the first glass of champagne for the first toast, which was given by Tom to his beautiful bride. Once they were back inside, many other toasts followed.

Though Hale wasn't surprised this minor miracle had been achieved, seeing as Nora was involved in the planning.

Now he and Elsa, Rix and Alex, along with Blake were lounged in one of the seating areas in the corner of the living room, and Rix was saying what they all were thinking.

Since they came in from the garden, Jamie had been casting irate glances at Nora, more than likely because she was avoiding him.

But more, something was going on between Sully and Dru.

That was a new one.

And if that wasn't enough, as had become usual, Cadence was wearing her heart on her sleeve for Gage.

Since Hale had known him, Gage had grown up a lot. He was more boy than man when Hale first met him. Now, he was a laidback guy who was quick with a joke, but considering he was close to finishing his master's in ecology and biodiversity, there was a serious side to him that was nowhere to be found back when the families first entwined.

Even so, Gage seemed entirely unaware of the fact that Cadence was into him in a huge way, and Hale sensed that wasn't because today wasn't the day for him to go there.

He sensed, and Cadence definitely sensed, it was because he thought of her more like a little sister than a possible girlfriend.

"Chloe says Sully and Dru started to be a thing at Judge's mom's funeral," Alex said quietly.

"Really?" Blake asked. "That long?"

Alex nodded. "Nothing happened, but Chloe said it was obvious they were into each other. And nothing has happened since, because Chloe believes Sully refuses to go there because of Judge."

"If it didn't work out, it could make things awkward," Elsa noted. "Same with Gage and Cadence."

"Cadence is simply out of luck," Alex shared. "Gage looks like he's oblivious, but he's not. Chloe told me that too. He's just not about to start a thing with someone he considers a stepsister, who he genuinely has feelings for as a sister, but nothing more. He's trying to get her in that headspace by treating her as such, she's just not following his lead."

"Bummer for her, Gage is a hottie," Elsa muttered, and sipped her fake wine spritzer.

Hale raised his brows to her.

"Obviously, no one is hotter than you," she assured.

"When it comes to you, I know that," Hale replied. "But I wouldn't have called Gage being your type."

"Tall, dark, built, smart, loving and determined to save fragile ecosystems?" she asked. "Have you met who I'm engaged to?"

Rix chuckled, Alex and Blake laughed.

But Hale smirked.

"I need to tap this gossip vein of Chloe's," she noted. "I'm seriously falling down on my job."

"Well, she knows it all," Alex replied. "She makes it her mission."

No change there.

"You two are next," Elsa remarked. "How is wedding planning going?"

Alex made a face. Rix suddenly looked pissed. And Blake sighed.

Elsa didn't miss any of it.

"What?" she pushed.

"Mother is a pill," Blake said as answer.

"Everything is set," Rix stated firmly, then he turned his attention to his woman. "So we can order the fucking invitations."

Alex bit her lip.

"You need to order the invitations, Alex," Blake pressed.

Alex said nothing.

"Spill," Elsa ordered.

"We're having the ceremony in Prescott," Rix decreed. Alex opened her mouth, but Rix bit out, *"Prescott."*

Oh shit.

Blake leaned toward Elsa and Hale and stage-whispered, "Mother is demanding it happen at the family estate in England."

"Really? Why?" Elsa queried.

"Because she's committed to the art of being difficult," Blake answered. "We spent time there when we were younger, but it isn't home. New York is where we grew up. And for Alex, Prescott is home now."

"What Blake isn't saying is that Ned is over her shit," Rix shared tightly. "She doesn't get under his skin anymore. And since Blake's right, she made an art of doing that for the last three decades, she's jonesing for a way to get her fix, and she's using my woman to aid that cause."

"They're having a small ceremony in Prescott, and it's going to be very pretty, if I do say so myself, since I'm planning it considering Alex isn't a wedding-planning type of person," Blake announced. "Then they're going on a three-week honeymoon, which I am *not* planning, Rix is. But when they get back, they're having a party here in New York for our people, mostly Dad's cronies."

"And that's what's going to happen," Rix said to Alex. "Because that's what *we* want, but also because my folks could make it, but most of my buds can't afford to fly across a continent and an ocean for the sole purpose of watching us get hitched."

"Maybe just a party there too," Alex suggested.

Rix blew out such a huge breath, Hale felt it fan the room.

More leaning and stage-whispering from Blake. "She's the family peacemaker."

"Mum just wants to be a part of it," Alex said stubbornly.

"No, my pushover of a sister," Blake denied. "She's perfectly capable of boarding a plane to Phoenix, then renting a car to drive herself to Prescott. What she wants is to be a pain in Dad's ass. And barring Dad, Rix's."

"She barely remembers Rix's name," Alex mumbled.

"Hello?" Blake called. "She does, she just pretends she doesn't so she can be a pain in *your* ass."

"Are we talking about Helena?" Chloe asked as she wedged her ass on the arm of Rix's chair.

"Is the temperature in this corner twenty degrees lower because her specter is hanging here?" Blake asked in return.

"No, it's twenty degrees hotter because Rix looks like he wants to strangle someone, and the only one I know he wants to strangle is Helena," Chloe replied.

"Fuck it," Rix said. "I'm ordering the invitations when we get home."

"No worries, my friend," Blake put in. "They're already designed and ready to roll. If I have the go ahead, I'll do it."

"You have the go ahead," Rix stated.

"Wait—" Alex tried.

"No more waiting," Rix gritted.

"But—" she tried again.

"If I corralled that pastor and made her marry us sitting right here, would you give a shit?" Rix asked.

"No," Alex answered.

"Do you care how we do it?" Rix pushed.

"Well, Chloe and Blake found me the perfect dress," she returned. "So, kinda, *yes.*"

"Does that dress say English garden wedding in June?" Rix kept at her.

"Not even close," Chloe shared.

Rix took his woman's hand and tugged on it so she was leaning over the arm of her chair and deep in his space.

"Baby, I get you," he said gently. "You got your sister back. Your dad. You're going for the trifecta. And I hate this for you, but there's no getting around it. It's not gonna happen."

When Rix said that, Blake turned her head to mask her emotion, but Hale didn't miss it.

And yeah.

That meant Blake got her sister back, and her dad, and it meant everything to her.

But Blake was Blake. She didn't want to let it show.

"She got what she wanted," Rix went on. "Your attention and your frustration. Enough. Let's get married, for fuck's sake."

Not the most romantic statement, but it worked on Alex, Hale knew, because her face got soft, and she whispered, "Okay, honey."

Rix kissed her.

She sat back and looked to her sister. "We'll order the invitations and announcements."

"*Finally*," Blake said dramatically.

"*My sister is pregnant?*"

Hale froze solid, he felt Elsa do the same at his side, and the attention of everyone in their cluster went across the room, then shot right back to Hale and Elsa after Emilie's words sounded in a shout from the dining room.

"*Emilie*," Hale heard David snap.

But Hale had no attention for David, seeing as he was rising from his chair because Emilie was charging across the space on a direct trajectory to Elsa.

"We need to take this outside," he growled when Elsa's sister arrived.

He didn't even have the chance to do a quick scan to see where Tom and Mika were, because Emilie was glaring murder at Elsa along with speaking.

"What is it with you?" Emilie demanded of Elsa.

"Again, we're taking this outside," Hale decreed.

Elsa rose out of her seat.

Emilie ignored Hale and her tone was snide when she said, "Big time job. Fame. Fortune. Rich fiancé. Now *you're having his baby* so *People* and TMZ can talk about how *perfect* you are and how *in love*."

Oskar was suddenly there, and he murmured to Hale, "I fucked up," before, to his sister, he said in a steely voice, "We're taking a walk, Em."

She ignored Oskar too, shouting, "*God*, can't you leave *anything for me?*"

Now David was there. "If you don't pipe down this minute—" he started to threaten.

Emilie whirled on him. "I'm not *twelve, Dad*."

"You could have fooled me," David retorted.

Emilie's torso swung back in affront.

"Please, let's move this outside," Elsa begged.

And rounding it out, now Inger was there, appearing hurt.

"Honey, why didn't you tell me?" she asked Elsa, sounding as hurt as she looked.

"We just found out," Elsa explained. "Dad guessed. I was going to call a family meeting imminently. I swear."

"Damn, Tom, Mika, I'm so sorry," David muttered, and Hale's gut sank.

Because they were now standing right there as well.

"You're having a baby?" Tom asked, his gaze shifting between Hale and Elsa.

"It wasn't planned, but we're thrilled," Hale told him. "We just got it confirmed, but we didn't want to steal the limelight on your day, even before we knew how big this day was going to be."

Hale noted vaguely Inger looked mollified that Tom didn't know, but mostly, his attention was on Tom, who was now studying his new wife closely.

"You knew?" he demanded.

"I was sworn to secrecy, Tommy," she replied. "We made a cocktail promise."

"Oh, well, there you go," Tom drawled. "I'm going to be a grandfather, and didn't know it because you made a cocktail promise."

Mika aimed a stretched-lips look to Nora, then Genny.

Not a good call.

"Both of you knew too?" Tom asked, his voice rising.

"Obviously, Elsa went to Genny first," Mika shared.

Way not a good call.

Inger gasped.

He heard Elsa sigh.

"Just to point out, this time, it wasn't me," Sasha chimed in.

Chloe didn't quite swallow her laugh in time for it to be inaudible.

Another not great call.

"Jesus, *everybody* knew?" Tom demanded of the room at large, a room that was now crowded with the entirety of their twenty-three guests, and the pastor.

"Tom, we thought you'd asked us here to announce your engagement," Hale informed him. "We were all happy for you and we wanted you both to have that without anything interfering."

"I have the capacity to feel a great deal of love and joy about a variety of things all at once, son," Tom retorted.

"I'll bear that in mind next time," Hale muttered.

"Are you seriously angry?" Mika inquired of her new husband.

Tom turned to his new wife. "Honey, when you're the last to know Cadence is having a baby, you tell me how you'd react."

"Valid," Mika muttered before she gave big eyes to Genny, who was one of the best actresses in the country, but at that moment, she was failing at fighting her smile.

"Oh for heaven's sake," Nora waded in, followed by the bartender and two of the catering staff, all of them holding trays of filled champagne glasses. "You two are married. Your ceremony was *life*. Everyone is thrilled for you. They're pregnant. They're happy. Now today is doubly joyous. Please, I beg you, get with the program."

She took one of the glasses that were being passed around and raised it.

"To love. To family. To friends. To the future. And to the best times of our lives shared in the greatest of company," she toasted.

There were some "hear, hears" and a few "cheers" and everyone lifted their glasses and drank.

Once that was done, Hale witnessed Tom giving Elsa a tight hug.

He then turned that on Hale.

"Thrilled for you, son," Tom whispered in his ear.

"Me too, Tommy," Hale replied. "And just in case you didn't get it, I'm thrilled for you too."

"Don't worry. I got it."

With that, Tom broke it off, did the pat on the face again, and it felt as good as the last time.

"I call the baby shower!" Blake shouted.

"Oh no you don't," Chloe snarled. "She's my sister-in-law. Or she's going to be. I get first dibs."

"What's that saying about snoozing and losing?" Blake drawled smugly.

"Ladies, *please*," Nora waded in again. "Obviously, Imogen, Mika and I are throwing the shower."

"I guess I'm chopped liver," Inger grumbled under her breath.

"No, dear," Nora purred, curving an arm around Inger's waist and drawing her away, but Hale heard her finish, "My apologies. We're a crew of four. Let's start brainstorming. With what I have in mind, we can't begin planning too soon. Allow me to share."

"Well, *ma sœur*, it's official now, you're going to have the best baby shower in history," Chloe decreed.

"But of course she is," Emilie hissed, before she announced to no one and everyone, "I'm leaving."

And then she stormed off rudely (since she didn't say goodbye to the happy couple), dramatically, and pitifully (since no one paid attention).

Oskar got close and said, "I'm an asshole. Dad told me, and I was just excited for you two. Obviously, I could have no idea Emilie would act like that."

Elsa's sister was a piece of work, but even Hale wouldn't have guessed she'd act like that.

"It's okay, Oskar," Elsa told him.

Oskar looked to Hale.

"It is, man. All good," Hale assured.

Oskar clapped him on the arm before he went in for a hug from his sister.

"See?" Sasha asked, staring pointedly at Chloe, Matt, Gage, Sully, and finally Hale, "I *can* keep a secret."

"Congratulations, Sash, you lasted seven whole hours," Matt teased.

Sasha rolled her eyes and flounced off.

Hale and Elsa sat back down.

Oskar dragged a chair over to sit with them.

And twenty minutes later, Tom and Mika cut their cake.

CHAPTER 8

ONLY YOU

Hale

ix weeks later...

THE ELEVATOR DOORS OPENED, AND AFTER HE WALKED OUT, HALE WAS greeted by his fiancée.

"Hey, baby," he murmured before he dropped his head to brush his lips against hers.

"Hey," she replied when he was finished. "I know we have to get ready, but come look really quick. I think I've got it licked."

She took his hand and he used his other one to pull his messenger bag over his head as she guided him to the kitchen island.

The minute he saw what was scattered all over it, that tightness he was living with reminded him of its presence with a vengeance, and it wasn't just in his neck this time, but along his shoulders, and lately, even down his back.

"I think we're going with blue," Elsa said as he dumped his bag on one of the stools at the island. "I don't go in for that blue is boys, pink is girls thing. Blue is tranquil. There are studies that suggest bedrooms should be blue, because it's a calming color. And we're probably going to need that. Not to mention, it's pretty. There'll be a lot of yellow and green to contrast. And this crib, as you can plainly see, is a *must*."

He stared down at paint chips, printed-out floor plans, pictures of baby furniture, mobiles and wall décor, and wallpaper samples.

It was six weeks after they got the confirmation, and Elsa was firmly out of the first trimester.

The minute she was, she engaged an interior designer to start work on the nursery.

They'd had their appointment with the doctor. Elsa had long since come off caffeine and had carved daily walks into her hectic schedule, sometimes doing it on the treadmill upstairs since the weather was getting chilly outside.

She'd had about two weeks of morning sickness, but that subsided. Occasionally, she'd still get nauseous, and even throw up. But it didn't last long, she handled it like she'd been experiencing it all of her life, and she just got on with shit.

Now, even though the danger zone never really passed, the most precarious part of it had, and it was time to get their shit tight because, with the hectic lives they lived, before they knew it, they'd have a baby.

Tom and Mika had landed in Phoenix after their honeymoon, and stayed there for a while.

They'd been back in New York for the last week, though, and tonight was the first time he and Elsa would see them. Also tonight there was an event for a breast cancer research facility in the city to which Jamie had bought a table (along with being a major sponsor), and they were all going.

But Hale hadn't shaken the feeling of trepidation he had that he didn't understand, because he was genuinely thrilled with what was soon to come for him and his woman.

So he didn't get it.

That meant, now that Tom was back, Hale needed to find time to hash things out with him.

It was just that Elsa was being Elsa.

She was firing on all cylinders.

The surprise of the news, and sharing it, having been accomplished, she threw herself headlong into planning their lives around their baby, both the run up to the arrival, and after.

Considering she wanted to take a solid six months off after the baby was born, she needed to get down to filming her next slate of interviews for the streaming contract she had. So she and her staff were busy rescheduling, researching and moving everything up by months.

This included her flying back and forth to LA twice in the last six weeks, and although sometimes before pregnancy, she'd go without him, these times, he had his assistants juggle his schedule so he could go with her.

Although this flurry of intense work alarmed him, Hale didn't say a word. If that was what she needed to do to feel stress-free and commit to their kid when he or she got there, he was behind it.

In fact, he had the same kind of thing happening, since they talked and agreed that, once she was back at work, Hale would take at least three months, but hopefully more like five or six, to take over when she returned to work. He just had a lot longer to make plans.

But all this was eating at him.

She was doing too much. He couldn't believe he had the thought, but he frequently had to catch himself from encouraging her to stop walking, simply to free up more time to do the other things.

She'd never been a nine-to-five woman. She was out of the penthouse early, he was usually home before her (though, he made a point of doing this so he could start cooking), and it wasn't a rare occurrence in the evenings she was working on the couch beside him doing the same.

Now, she'd added dealing with this nursery.

It was too much, and it didn't seem to be slowing down.

"You hate it," she said, taking his attention back to her.

He focused on the grouping of paint chips, furniture and décor pictures, and the wallpaper sample she'd assembled for his perusal.

She was right. He wasn't sure he'd ever paid attention to a baby crib in his life, or even seen one.

But that one was the shit.

"No, baby, it's perfect," he replied, and it wasn't a lie, it was.

"Your face didn't say that two seconds ago," she commented, her focus acute on him, as he'd been noticing often in the past six weeks it had been.

He looked to her, and again, didn't lie.

Exactly.

"It's just been a long day."

"We can cancel tonight. I'm sure Jamie won't mind."

"They're renaming the research facility the Rosalind Oakley Center for Breast Cancer Research," Hale reminded her. "This is a big deal for him. And Dru, who was on the planning committee. I think he'd mind."

She scrunched her face to concede the point.

That made some of the tension ebb away, and he bent to kiss her forehead before he lifted up and said something he really didn't want to say, "Paul's picking us up in an hour, sweetheart."

"Drat!" she cried, leaned up to kiss his jaw, then she dashed up the stairs.

Frosty dashed with her.

Frosty needed the exercise.

But Hale sure as fuck wished his woman wouldn't run up the stairs.

Cheddar jumped on the island, taking his attention at the same time scattering paint chips, then standing at the edge of the counter and staring at them as they floated to the floor.

He started purring when Hale reached out and scratched his neck.

"What's my mind fuck, kitten?" he asked the cat.

Cheddar looked to him and meowed, but regrettably, it wasn't an answer to his question.

It was a demand for treats.

At that point, even though it was a priority he figured his shit out, Hale had no choice.

One of the babies he already had needed treats.

So he got on that.

He'd pulled his shit together, mostly because, when Elsa emerged from transforming herself from daytime, busy celebrity journalist to nighttime socialite, he couldn't think of anything else.

Chloe was dressing her these days, and the gown that she'd sent for this event—which was black with big bursts of shimmering champagnes and golds, strapless but with a plunging neckline, the skirt full but a slit ran up near to her hip on one side—was perfect for her. Elegant, sophisticated, but still racy and daring.

It was when Paul crept up to where they'd be let out on the red carpet, and he saw the crush and the flashbulbs popping, that something happened Hale had never experienced.

He was finding it difficult to breathe.

He saw Hudson turn his head and lock eyes with him, so he knew whatever he was experiencing he was putting out into the car.

He also knew that Rocco, Elsa's bodyguard, was already at the event. He would meet them at their arrival, but he'd do that after he'd taken a lay of the land.

"Paul, don't stop, keep going," Elsa ordered.

Yep.

Whatever he was feeling, he was putting out there.

"Paul, stick with the plan," Hale contradicted her order.

"Something's up with you," Elsa stated like an accusation.

He turned to her. "You know I hate this shit."

"I do, but it's not that."

It wasn't that.

"I'll be fine once we get inside."

She glared at him, but he knew, even in the dark car, she wasn't missing anything.

"This is important to Jamie. It's important we show up, have our pictures taken and bring awareness to this issue," he said.

"It isn't like breast cancer doesn't have awareness, Hale," she retorted.

"It also doesn't have a cure."

That got her. He could tell when her mouth screwed up in annoyance.

"I'm fine, sweetheart. Promise."

Another lie.

Fuck him.

With that, she said to Hudson, "Double time on the step and repeat. Move us along fast, Hud, and get us inside, please."

"Gotcha. I'll text Rocco," Hudson muttered.

Elsa turned away from him to look out her window, and he felt like a dick, because he was lying, and she knew it.

Christ, he had to talk to Tom.

Things didn't get better as it became their turn to hit the red carpet.

Rocco was there to open the door, Hudson got out in a flash, and one lie he didn't tell, he hated this shit. The lights flashing. The questions shouted. The press of people.

But this time, it wasn't simply something he detested.

From the instant he alighted behind Elsa, it was torture.

As they moved along, he knew his fingers were crushing hers, he just couldn't stop them.

Until he let her go, but he did this only to snake an arm around her waist and yank her so close to his side, they had to walk like they were in a three-legged race as they endured the step and repeat.

Hudson and Rocco moved them along quickly, but Hale didn't hear a single question called to them. He got an instant headache trying to scan every face, his entire reason for being set on trying to feel if there was some threat. Every flash exploding felt like a bullet he had to protect her from, so remaining standing with Elsa tucked to his side like targets was agony.

He didn't know if Elsa gave Hudson and Rocco a sign, or if they felt it, but the last stop on the carpet in front of the backdrop lasted approximately two seconds before the two men converged and practically shoved them inside.

The tightness in his chest immediately released.

Elsa immediately confronted him.

"You need to learn to open up to me," she snapped, keeping her voice low as they were surrounded by a milling crowd.

"We'll talk. Later," he promised.

"Really?" she asked sarcastically. "Because whatever this is, Hale, started when I told you we were expecting, and it's been getting worse since. And I gotta say, it doesn't feel all that great, not only you trying to hide whatever is going on with you, but that whatever it is has to do with our baby."

After delivering that, she glided away in a huff that stated clearly he was not to follow, Rocco trailing her.

"Fuck," Hale said under his breath.

"It's the kid," Hudson said under his.

Hale turned to his man. "Sorry?"

"Dude, it's bad enough when it's just her. It got worse when we screwed the pooch and she got cut. But now, you got a kid coming, so it's no surprise this shit went into overdrive for you. I get it. It would do the same to me too."

Holy.

Fuck.

That was it.

How hadn't he seen it?

"I got no advice," Hudson went on. "But who you two are is never going to change, Hale. We fucked up, but that shit is not gonna happen again. I know that doesn't make it better, and it doesn't make you feel she's safer in the now. You two making a family, like I said, I get it. It's far worse. But, even though I know I don't gotta tell you this, I'm gonna say it. You have no choice but to figure it out."

"You've already helped, Hud."

Hudson looked to the crowd and muttered, "Glad to hear it."

Hale blew out a breath, and he couldn't say he was over it.

But he could say that he was pleased as all hell to finally know what "it" was, because now he could tackle dealing with it.

Another reason Hale hated these things happened right then, when it took him half an hour to find Tom because so many people stopped him for a greeting, or a moment of ingratiation.

But finally, he made it to Tom, who was thankfully standing only with Ned.

"Son," Tom greeted with a smile, giving him a hug.

He returned it, shook hands with Ned, and Tom spoke again.

"First, you don't have a drink. And second, but more importantly, you don't have your fiancée. Is Elsa here?"

"She's here and she's pissed at me," Hale shared. And then, because it had been festering so long, he had to release it, he laid it out. "I'm not opening up about the abject terror that's been building in me since she told me she was pregnant considering I am powerless to keep her and our child safe from all the whackjobs out there."

Tom's head ticked sharply at this quick sharing of honesty, as it would. Hale hadn't even asked about his honeymoon, or Mika.

Ned cleared his throat and asked, "Would you like me to leave?"

"No," Hale told him. "You're a father. And both your daughters get media attention. So I think you understand me."

"I very much do," Ned murmured.

Hale turned back to Tom, and he *still* didn't ask about the honeymoon or Tom's new bride.

He kept laying it out.

"That said, until Hudson pointed it out, I didn't realize that was my problem. I just felt guilt that something negative was happening in my head when something so positive was happening in my life."

"You do know, like Ned, I have some experience with this, Hale," Tom pointed out carefully.

"Well, since I didn't know what was fucking with me, I couldn't talk to you about it either. Now that you're back in the city, I'd planned to connect with you to hash it out."

"Let's do that tomorrow as a priority. Mika and I'll have you both over for dinner," Tom invited.

"Appreciated," Hale muttered. And louder, he added, "And I look forward to hearing about your honeymoon."

"There isn't much to say. I'm sure Bora Bora is lovely," Tom replied. "Though Mika and I didn't see much of it."

That mean the honeymoon wasn't good.

It was great.

Hale relaxed slightly and shot Tom a smile.

"Elsa is angry now, but when she knows the issue, she won't be," Ned put in, perhaps sensing Hale was still tense. "You know that, don't you?"

"It makes me feel weak," Hale admitted.

Ned's brows shot together. "Because you want to protect your woman and your child?"

"Because I wasn't smart enough to figure out what was going on with me until it got to the point my woman got pissed at me because she hasn't missed it, and now she thinks I have some reservations about starting our family," Hale explained.

"This begs the question of why you're now talking to us instead of her," Ned replied.

"Because Elsa needs to flare out," Hale told him. "We both have quick tempers. But fortunately, that means they don't last long."

"Ah," Ned said on a grin.

"It'll be okay, Hale," Tom said with reassurance.

"You can't know that," Hale returned.

"What I know is, you don't have any control over it. So you have to find a way not to let it control you." Tom shook his head. "Not for now. We'll talk tomorrow. Now…incoming."

Hale turned because Tom's gaze had drifted over his shoulder, and he saw Elsa and Mika approaching.

He kissed Mika's cheek then took his woman's hand.

She glowered at him.

Right then.

Not over it yet.

Well…

Tough.

He couldn't have her thinking he had issues with their growing family, so he was going to see to that directly.

"If you'll excuse us," he said, and pulled her to a deserted alcove.

"Just so you know, I've bid approximately one point seven million dollars on silent auction items," she declared when he boxed her into the space with his back to the room.

"I don't give a fuck."

"I overbid significantly, so it's unlikely anyone will outbid me."

"I'll repeat, I don't give a fuck."

"One of them is a diamond necklace," she shared tartly. "And in case you aren't getting this, you'll be writing the check when I win."

"One minute, you were sitting beside me and smiling. Ten minutes later, you were sitting by the basin in a men's restroom, covered in blood."

Her face grew slack with shock, then soft with understanding.

"Handsome," she whispered.

"The second I saw you in that bathroom, I had an overwhelming surge of different emotions. Terror. Concern. Guilt. Anger. It was too much. I couldn't cope."

"I know," she said gently.

"Now, if something happened to you while you're carrying our child. Or something happens to our child once she's with us, I wouldn't be able to deal."

She sidled close to him in order to tuck herself to his front. "You would, Hale."

"No, Elsa, I would not. There's not another woman on this earth who is meant for me. There is no Mika. There is no Nora once Jamie sorts his shit. It's you. Only you. And the baby we make…"

He couldn't finish that.

She lifted a hand to cup his jaw. "Honey, why didn't you tell me this was on your mind?"

"Because I couldn't figure out what was wrong with me," he explained. "I was happy, and I was freaked way the fuck out, and I felt shame because I was freaked out, even if I didn't know why."

"All this is understandable."

"I know that *now*. Until Hudson diagnosed my condition half an hour ago, I didn't know it."

"Hudson gets a raise," she decreed.

He couldn't believe it, but that urged a smile to his lips.

"And you need to talk to Tom," she advised.

"I already have. We're going there for dinner tomorrow night."

Hale saw her relax, so he wrapped his arms around her.

"I'm sorry I—" he began.

"Stop it, honey. You got there in the end."

He shut up.

"I don't think I can change my bids," she warned.

Only Elsa could make him laugh after all of that, something she did.

"Canoodling in a corner, of course."

They turned in the direction of a familiar voice and saw Dru standing there, smiling brightly at them, her flame-red hair in an updo, her column gown stunning.

"I hate to break this up," she continued, "but we're sitting, and I need all the help I can get to break the tension, because Roland is here, and Nora is annoyed, but Dad is super pissed."

Roland was Nora's ex-husband, and it hadn't been lost on any of them, particularly Jamie, that he'd been sniffing around Nora for months now.

"Interesting," Elsa said under her breath.

"I wish Dad would just go there and put a stop to this," Dru groused. "He's being supremely aggravating."

Hale and Elsa exchanged a glance at that, because of all of the crew, Dru was the only one they didn't know if Nora had her blessing, and it simply wasn't right to ask a daughter who lost her mother if she was okay with her dad having another woman in his life. Even Elsa couldn't figure out how to wring that info from her.

But they had the answer to that now.

"Anyway!" Dru cried brightly. "See you in there." She made to take off but turned back and said, "Oh, and thanks for that huge bid on the necklace, Elz. Wow! Amazing! And it'll look stunning on you."

Only then did she spirit away.

Hale tucked his woman's hand in his elbow and drew them out of the alcove, asking, "How large was your bid on that?"

"Don't ask, just pray for a cure."

Her answer meant, when they walked into the ballroom where the dinner had been set up, all his tension was gone.

And Hale was laughing.

Hard.

CHAPTER 9

THRIVING

Hale

The next night, they'd assumed their customary after-dinner places when he and Elsa went to Tom and Mika's for dinner.

As had become customary, Tom and Hale were in armchairs at the back of the long living room. Mika and Elsa were also in their usual places when he and his woman came for dinner. They were cackling with each other on a couch at the front.

However, this time, he wouldn't have to pour Elsa in the car due to her level of inebriation because the women weren't downing after-dinner cocktails like it was an event in the Olympics and they were in training. And Mika, being her usual awesome, wasn't imbibing because Elsa couldn't.

Tom started it.

"You seem better."

He tore his focus off his fiancée and looked to Tom.

"It's a relief to know what it is," he shared. "I sat down with Heath today." (Heath was his head of security.) "And I told him where my head was at. He wasn't surprised. And he assured me, since I told

them the news, they'd already begun preparatory planning and training, whatever that means for them. I didn't ask. He didn't offer the
info. We were both good with that. But it made me feel a little better.
He also told me he wanted another person on our security team, and
whoever has the baby with them has two people on them. He then
strongly advised that we keep this up until the kid is at least fifteen or
sixteen, if we're all together or she's with one of us, two guards. But
definitely, once the baby is old enough to go out and do stuff herself,
she has her own bodyguard, something he didn't need to tell me. That
was a given."

"She?" Tom asked.

Hale felt his lips quirk. "I'm manifesting."

Tom chuckled.

"She hasn't admitted it, but Elsa is manifesting something else, and
I think she has the upper hand," Hale remarked.

"Sadly for you both, genetics have the upper hand," Tom reminded
him.

Hale shrugged good-naturedly and took a sip of his bourbon.

"I'm pleased you're tackling the things you need to tackle," Tom
said. "It lends a sense of control."

"Mm," Hale murmured in agreement.

"I'm sad to say, the concern doesn't ever go away."

Hale's mellow mood fled.

"You get used to it," Tom added. "But it doesn't go away."

"Brilliant," Hale groused.

"Hale." Tom said his name in a way that Hale's focus on him inten-
sified. "A lot is happening in your life. Your business. Your mission.
Falling in love. Being engaged. Having a baby. Genny with Duncan.
Me with Mika. New family members. Chloe finding Judge. Your dad."

Hale drew in a breath and held it.

And Tom carried on.

"I remind you of all of this because it's important to have done so
when I say what I'm going to say next. This being, that concern never
going away isn't about stalkers and photographers. It's about being a
parent."

Hale let the breath out in a whoosh.

Tom kept speaking.

"I can understand that didn't occur to you, and why, the reason for that something I just explained. But even if you weren't you, and Elsa wasn't Elsa, you'd be worried about everything under the sun, and finding some way to protect your child from it."

"Christ, I'm slow on the uptake," he muttered irritably.

"No you aren't. Chloe was three years old, and Matt closing on two, before Marilyn took me aside and reamed my ass for being an overbearing father. I contradicted her, telling her I was overprotective, that was different, and it wasn't a bad thing. She wasn't hearing it and stated that overprotective *was* overbearing, the first was how I thought about it, the second was how Chloe and Matt would eventually feel about it. And they wouldn't thank me for it. She then told me I needed to sort myself out and let my daughter and son grow and thrive and ultimately make their own decisions and live their lives."

This time, it was Tom who took in a big breath, before he leaned Hale's way and continued talking.

"You are not unique in this, son. You aren't an outlier or weak. I believe every father, or at least the good ones, go through this in some form or other when they first learn that role is in their future. Your situation was exacerbated by what happened to Elsa. But you aren't alone in this. And like many other things that don't feel good, but in reality are, the depth of emotion you have around this bodes good things for your child."

"Thanks, Tommy," Hale whispered, because that made sense, he was so deep in his own head it didn't occur to him, and it was good to have it out there.

"Don't thank me yet, that was the easy part."

That was easy?

"Shit," Hale bit off.

Tom didn't hesitate. "I can't know, he didn't explain it to me, but since last night, when you shared what was going on with you, and since you opened the box—"

Hale's spine snapped straight at mention of the box his dad gave him.

"—it's hit me this is undoubtedly something Corey felt too. This overwhelming need to protect you. Understanding his fame, and for him, his fortune, and how vulnerable you were to both, augmenting that with the enormous burden he carried that his parents gave him, it makes me wonder if his distance from you, distance he fostered between the two of you, had something to do with this same thing."

"Jesus," Hale muttered, Tom's words making him feel like his chest had hollowed out.

"Again, I don't know, but it makes sense. And outside of Genny, Corey was an island. He didn't share much with anybody, including, it would turn out, Genny. But I think with this, when his parents were the threat his entire life, he had no idea what to do with that overpowering need to protect. He wouldn't know it's natural in all parents. He might have even thought the strength of what he was experiencing was a threat to you. For once in his genius life, there was something he simply didn't know. And regrettably, he didn't ask."

Hale sat back and took another sip of his bourbon, his gaze drifting to Elsa who was leaned into Mika, looking at something on Mika's phone.

"Hale," Tom called.

Hale didn't take his attention from Elsa as he said quietly, "I heard you, Tom. And yes, you're correct. That makes sense."

"Now."

Tom saying that one word and nothing more had Hale looking at him.

"Now?" he asked after it.

"Now. You're my son, if not my blood, and this is a for instance. Now, I feel helpless to protect you from the emotion you're feeling, and it guts me completely."

"God, Tommy," Hale whispered, feeling gutted himself.

"Here's the thing," Tom continued. "I welcome it, because I have you. It's just another form of love, Hale. It's heartbreaking your dad didn't have an example to turn to in order to understand what he was experiencing. But even if he didn't get it, he *was* feeling love. And that's a beautiful thing."

"We need to stop talking about this now," Hale warned gruffly.

"I hear you," Tom replied and gave him what he asked for by sitting back.

"You mean the world to me," Hale told him.

"I know," Tom replied.

"You're going to be a great granddad."

Tom smiled. "I know that too."

"I don't know how to thank you for all you give to me," Hale admitted.

"Well, that's a thing too. Because you will, you just won't know it, because what I give you, you'll give your child, and that's all the thanks I'll need."

Jesus.

"We *really* need to stop talking now," Hale asserted.

Tom chuckled.

They lapsed onto other subjects, until, undoubtedly sensing the important stuff was done, Elsa called, "Handsome, get over here. You have to see Mika's pictures of their honeymoon."

So that was what they were looking at on Mika's phone.

"Coming," he called in return while pushing out of his chair.

Tom came up with him, and Hale made a move to head the women's way, but stopped when Tom caught his biceps.

"He knew you would thrive," Tom said low. "So before he left us, that was all he needed."

Hale swallowed hard.

"Now, I'm done," Tom said.

"Thank fuck."

Tom grinned at him.

Hale drew a big breath into his nose, let it out, and he and Tom went to go sit with the women so Hale could look at honeymoon pictures.

"IT'S CLEAR TO ME TOM SHOULD HAVE GONE INTO PSYCHOLOGY, NOT sports medicine."

It was later.

They were in bed, cuddling after making love and cleaning up. They had two cats at their feet, which would change once they fell asleep. Frosty would snuggle somewhere into Elsa's body. Cheddar would curl into himself beside Hale on Hale's pillow.

And he'd just told her about his conversation with Tom.

"Don't tell him that. He'll start applying to schools," Hale warned.

"Maybe I should and he'll get into a school in New York so we have them all the time and won't lose them to Phoenix every few weeks."

"Don't tell that to Chloe, or she'll swear a vendetta against you."

Elsa laughed softly.

They were both mellow, shit was sorted (for now).

It was time to hit something else.

"I need to tell you something that's concerning me."

"Sock it to me," she offered.

He smiled at her, but it faded before he said, "The pace you're keeping isn't sitting great with me."

"The pace?" she asked.

"Your usual hell bent for leather, but now, it's that and then some."

Understanding softened her body against his. "Hale, you don't need to worry."

"I know I don't. I know you're an intelligent woman and would never do anything to harm yourself or our child. But you need to know where I am with that."

Lines formed between her brows and she queried, "How much is this bugging you?"

"One thing I want a moratorium on is you running up the stairs."

"Honey," she murmured, now her body melted into his.

"No," he amended, "two things. Your obstetrician is here, so we'll be having the baby here, but I'd really like you to consider curtailing travel as soon as you can. I know you have some interviews set up in LA. But once that project is finished, I'd like for us to nest in New

York for a while. As easy as it is for us to be able to fly private, travel still takes it out of you. You're providing energy for two. The frequent back and forth to LA concerns me."

"I have two trips already scheduled," she reminded him.

"I know, and I'm not asking you to cancel. Just not schedule any more until the baby is cleared to fly."

She was watching him closely, but she said nothing.

"I'm good," Hale assured her. "It's okay. I'm being overprotective. I'll settle in. And your pace will slow, because you won't have any choice in that. Just, please, don't run up the stairs again." He paused and added, "Or down them. Or anywhere. Can you promise that?"

"I can promise that. I can also nest in New York, no problem," she said softly, came in to touch her lips to his, before she pulled away, but pressed closer and asked, "You feeling better about all of this?"

"I don't feel like a fucked-up mess, since all new fathers are fucked-up messes, apparently."

"At least that's progress," she joked.

He started stroking her back and assured, "I'm fine, baby. Really this time."

"Okay," she mumbled.

"And I'll do better at figuring my shit out before it affects you," he promised.

She sighed heavily before she ordered, "Hale, stop it."

He was confused. "Stop what?"

She pressed a hand into his chest. "I love *you*. I love you messed up. I love you when you're together. I love you when you're feeding Cheddar treats on the counter and it's irritating the living daylights out of me. I love you when you keep calling him, that being our unborn child, a her."

He cut in at that. "She *is* a her."

"Whatever," she returned. "Stop apologizing for being you."

He gathered her even closer. "Okay, baby."

"Yeesh," she pushed out.

"It's done. Get over it," he ordered.

"I also love you when you're being a bossman."

"I know that for certain," he teased, slipping his hand around to cup her breast.

She arched into his touch.

"Again?" he whispered.

"You have to ask?"

No.

He didn't.

He rolled into her.

And Frosty and Cheddar had to wait to settle in for the night because Mom and Dad were going at each other as usual, and taking their time doing it.

Once they were done, and Elsa's warm, soft body was tucked to his, her breaths deep and even, fast asleep, Hale drifted to sleep as well.

EPILOGUE

AND THOSE NOT

Hale

wo months (plus) later...

MIDWAY THROUGH THE FESTIVITIES, WHICH UNFORTUNATELY HE WAS ordered to attend, but fortunately, there were no games or ridiculous shit like that involved, his woman grabbed his hand and marched him into Nora's kitchen.

It was the week after Christmas, just days before the New Year.

A light snow was falling outside.

And they were at their baby shower.

Once they hit the kitchen, Hale looked around with interest.

He and Elsa had a great kitchen, but Nora's acres of green marble countertops, plethora of cabinets, including glass front ones up top that showed off how ludicrously organized her housekeeper or chef was, immediately captured Hale's attention.

Now that the nursery was done, maybe they needed a revamp of their kitchen. Nora's was galley, due to the age of her unit, its blueprint, and the space her kitchen was allotted, which was large, though narrow.

But she had a seven burner stove and two fridges and—

"Handsome," Elsa clipped.

He looked down at her.

She was a mixture of angry and pouting.

He knew why.

Though, he faked that he didn't.

"What?"

"Do you want to tell me what's going on?" she demanded.

Hale sidestepped one of Nora's catering staff before he replied, "We're in the midst of our baby shower, sweetheart, which means, as the guests of honor, we shouldn't be holed up in the kitchen."

"That's not what I'm talking about."

More faking. "What are you talking about?"

"Hale."

"Elsa."

"Handsome."

"Gorgeous."

Her ice-blue eyes drilled into him.

Hale kept his mouth shut.

"I'm not going back out there until you tell me what's going on which means *you* will have to go out there and open all those presents in front of everybody…*alone*," she threatened.

"You wouldn't do that to me," he said with mock gravity.

"If I must, I'll ask Paul to come get me, and not come back and get you until midnight."

"I know how to use the subway, Elsa."

"Spill it, Hale Wheeler."

He sighed.

She crossed her arms on her chest.

This took his attention to her baby bump, which was what he still called it, even if, now, it was a lot larger than a bump.

It was then he asked, "Are you okay that Emilie blew off the shower?"

She squinted her eyes at him. "You're deflecting."

"Answer me."

"No, I'm not okay," she stated. "She can be a pain, but her not showing is just bitchy. It's also unacceptable. But it will remain to be seen if it's unforgiveable."

"She's out of the running for godmother," Hale grumbled irately.

"Jews don't have godmothers," she reminded him. "And if we did, she was never in."

"Who were you thinking?" he asked curiously.

"I'm lucky I don't have to pick, because Carole would never forgive me if I picked Fliss. Fliss would never forgive me if I picked Carole. And Chloe and Sasha would never forgive you if we picked someone else."

"More reason to convert," Hale noted.

"Hale," she said in warning.

Well.

Shit.

"She doesn't want to steal your thunder, but Chloe's pregnant."

Her eyes got big, then for a woman who had very swollen feet, she moved fast.

So fast, she was out of the kitchen before he could catch her.

He followed her quickly, but she was on Chloe before he could stop her.

"You're pregnant?" she asked his sister.

Chloe looked to Hale and her eyes narrowed.

"Oh my God. Now *you* have a big mouth." She threw up her hands with exasperation. "Where does it end?"

"You're pregnant," Elsa said in a quiet voice.

Chloe looked back to her.

She barely got her eyes on Hale's woman before Elsa dragged her out of her seat with both hands capturing Chloe's and started girlie jumping, shaking Chloe's arms, and crying, "Skiing lessons!"

Chloe started bouncing too and shouted, "Soccer games!"

As an aside, it was official.

He'd been correct. Elsa had the upper hand. Because they'd had their ultrasound, and there was no mistaking they were having a boy.

Though Chloe was only late in her second month, so she and Judge had no idea yet.

Elsa didn't let go of Chloe when she turned to Hale and demanded, "Now we're definitely getting another plane."

Allow a woman during a tiff to spend three times as much for a diamond necklace than it was worth, the next thing she'll want was an extra plane.

Though, that diamond necklace looked stunning around her throat.

Even so.

"My son is not flying back and forth across the country to attend soccer practice every day with Chloe and Judge's offspring," Hale decreed.

Elsa leaned into Chloe and whispered loudly, "I'll work on him."

Hale found the first father in the crowd, that being Duncan, and he asked, "Are they all irrational in this state?"

"I'm not answering that," Duncan replied, but he did it smiling.

Elsa finally let Chloe go, whirled on Sasha, and shouted, "I get to throw the baby shower!"

"No way!" Sasha shouted back.

"I called it!" Elsa retorted.

"Baby, you'll have *our* baby by then," Hale reminded her.

"So?" she returned.

Pure Elsa.

Nothing slowed her down.

"You can co-throw it," Chloe said. "But please, God, no macramé, no offense to all the boho babes in attendance."

"None taken," Mika murmured, the words vibrating with her laughter.

"We're going to have it in Prescott, and Prescott *screams* boho," Sasha returned.

"I may live there, but my wellingtons are Chanel," Chloe shot back.

"Perhaps we should open presents," Inger suggested, firmly taking the attention off Chloe and Judge's good news, and landing it on her daughter.

Hale's phone vibrated, he took it out and read the text from Matt.

How's it going?

E made me spill. Throwdown between her and S for who gets C's shower. They're co-throwing it, he replied

I cannot tell you how glad I am I'm neck deep in horse shit.

Hale chuckled and sent a thumbs up emoji.

"I'm afraid you're going to have to sit over there and oo and ah over things you care not a whit about as Elsa opens the presents," Nora drawled in his ear.

He looked down at her and joked, "Did I do something to be punished for?"

"You got nothing but the good stuff. She pays for it for nine months then however long it takes her to recover. So...yes," she answered.

He couldn't argue that.

So he didn't.

He moved to the armchair next to Elsa's and sat down.

She leaned his way the minute he did in order to whisper, "Dad, Oskar, Jamie and Tom drifted into the library about ten minutes ago, and Duncan is fading in that direction. Judge is only staying to provide moral support to you, and would probably give one of his kidneys for an excuse to miss this. You want me to cover for you? You can take Judge and run."

"Baby, I wouldn't miss this for the world," he bald-faced lied.

She knew he was doing it, which was why she rolled her eyes.

Then she pasted a smile on her face because Inger was passing her the first present.

THREE AND A HALF MONTHS LATER...

HALE HAD THE STRAP OF THE DIAPER BAG OVER HIS SHOULDER AND THE baby in his carrier gripped in his hand.

Elsa carried in nothing but herself, which was good, because, even if she'd only been in the hospital two days, the cats were on her like she'd been gone a year.

Hale watched carefully as she went slowly when she bent to give them love.

Ascertaining she was good, he dumped the diaper bag on an armchair, put the carrier on the coffee table, unbuckled the straps and carefully lifted his newborn son to his shoulder.

"How much did that kill you?" Elsa asked, and he turned to see she was holding Frosty much like he was holding Laird.

"How much did what kill me?"

"Not being able to hold him for the entire trip back from the hospital."

He grinned at her.

Taking her man and her boy in, her face got soft, before her eyes again lifted to his.

"You didn't have to take a month off, honey. Mika said she and Tom aren't going to Arizona for a while, just in case we need some help. Mom is beside herself, and since she first laid eyes on our boy last night, she's asked me a hundred times when she gets to babysit. Fliss and Carole are in to help. Even Blake said she'd be around if we needed anything, though the caveat to that was emergency shopping. In other words, I've got support."

"And I've got a job where I can take six weeks off," he returned.

She tipped her head to the side. "I thought it was a month."

"It became six weeks at 5:27 last night," he replied, rubbing circles on Laird's back. "And it might become two months in about two seconds."

Her mouth twitched, and she shrugged off her jacket, threw it on the back of the chair and headed to the kitchen.

He was about to go to the diaper bag to get a blanket to drape over his boy when he saw her stop dead.

She was staring at something in the kitchen, so he looked that way.

When he saw the small white box with a wide, baby-blue satin ribbon wrapped around it, that was when he stilled.

"We should have known," Elsa said softly, so he tore his gaze off the box and looked at her to see her gaze, tender and warm, on him.

No one could get past the security in their building to get into this unit without them knowing.

No one.

But Rhys Vaughan.

"Open it," he ordered, his voice so throaty, it was nearly guttural.

She didn't go to the box.

She came to him, put her hand on Laird's back and ordered gently, "Give him to me."

"Elz—"

"Hale, go see what your father gave our son."

He swallowed, transferred Laird to her shoulder, then, when his boy was settled and she had him, he put his hand to the small of her back and guided her with him to the box.

It was sitting on an envelope.

Hale clenched his teeth and took the box off the envelope.

And there it was.

His father's handwriting.

Hale.

"I love this man," Elsa whispered reverently. When she noticed his inaction, she looked up at him and advised, "The box first, handsome."

He nodded and grabbed the present, tugging at the ribbon.

It fell away, and he opened the white package which exposed a Tiffany blue box. He pulled the Tiffany's box out of its container and opened it to see a sterling silver baby rattle.

"It's inscribed," Elsa noted quietly.

He pulled the rattle out, and breathing carefully, he read what was inscribed around one end of the rattle.

To, Laird Corey Thomas Wheeler.

He then looked at the other end.

From, Grandpa.

Hale made an animal noise that came from deep in his throat and shared the exquisite pain he was feeling, so Elsa with Laird crowded him.

"The envelope, honey," Elsa prompted, love in her tone, and urgency.

She was right.

Get it done.

And then deal so this could start to feel good, beautiful, right, instead of feeling like loss.

He pushed out a breath, took in another one, set the rattle back in its box and nabbed the envelope.

He slit it open with a finger and pulled out a notecard, the stock of which he'd seen before.

It had his father's name embossed at the top in black.

And his handwriting filling the white underneath.

> *Hale,*
>
> *My wish for you in this moment is to be a strong enough man never to hesitate showing your love and affection.*
>
> *And a smart enough one never to waste a moment.*
>
> *Proud of you.*
>
> *Happy for you.*
>
> *All my love,*
>
> *-Dad*

A pained breath exploded from him, and Elsa and Laird were in his arms.

Their boy, safe and snug, healthy and whole, was tucked between them.

Their love, and the love of their families and friends—those with them, and those not—on a blustery, spring day in New York City, warmed them all the way down to their souls.

Elsa

Four months later...

I woke with no man at my side.

Nor any cats.

When I looked to the smart home screen on Hale's bedside table, I saw I'd slept in.

So after I threw the covers back, hit the bathroom, did my mourning routine and walked into the hall, I didn't even bother going to the nursery next door.

By now, after a week in LA, I knew the drill.

I went downstairs and right to the kitchen.

Frosty and Cheddar had obviously had their morning wet food (and Cheddar had done his zoomies), because they were curled up together in an armchair, sleeping. Neither even raised their heads when I walked through the space.

One could say our fur babies loved LA.

After I grabbed myself a cup of decaf, along with noting the spent baby bottle by the sink (I pumped so Hale could feed and bond with our boy), I walked out on the balcony.

And there they were, where I knew they'd be.

Father and son, on the beach.

The sea breeze was ruffling Hale's dark brown hair.

Laird was strapped to his chest.

He wasn't doing anything but walking in and out of the waves that lapped the shore, Laird's arms and legs waving and pumping with excitement.

Both my boys loved the beach.

I settled in with my coffee and watched.

This happened every morning since we'd come to LA, and I never interfered.

Father-and-son time was important.

It didn't take long before Hale turned and started toward the stairs that led up to the house.

As usual, he looked up and saw me.

He lifted a hand to wave.

My baby boy bounced in his carrier.

Hale headed to the steps.

I looked to the ocean.

"Thank you," I whispered.

The sea had nothing to say, nor did the man who gave us this view to it, but its breeze lifted the hair off my neck.

I heard Hale and Laird come in from outside.

So I was content with that reply.

Thus, I headed inside.

The End

The River Rain Saga will continue with Embracing the Change, coming September 10, 2024.

LEARN MORE ABOUT KRISTEN ASHLEY'S RIVER RAIN SERIES

After the Climb: A River Rain Novel, Book 1

They were the Three Amigos: Duncan Holloway, Imogen Swan and Corey Szabo. Two young boys with difficult lives at home banding together with a cool girl who didn't mind mucking through the mud on their hikes.

They grew up to be Duncan Holloway, activist, CEO and face of the popular River Rain outdoor stores, Imogen Swan, award-winning actress and America's sweetheart, and Corey Szabo, ruthless tech billionaire.

Rich and very famous, they would learn the devastating knowledge of how the selfish acts of one would affect all their lives.

And the lives of those they loved.

Start the River Rain series with After the Climb, the story of Duncan and Imogen navigating their way back to each other, decades after a fierce betrayal.

And introduce yourself to their families, who will have their stories told when River Rain continues.

Chasing Serenity: A River Rain Novel, Book 2

From a very young age, Chloe Pierce was trained to look after the ones she loved.

And she was trained by the best.

But when the man who looked after her was no longer there, Chloe is cast adrift—just as the very foundation of her life crumbled to pieces.

Then she runs into tall, lanky, unpretentious Judge Oakley, her exact opposite. She shops. He hikes. She drinks pink ladies. He drinks beer. She's a city girl. He's a mountain guy.

Obviously, this means they have a blowout fight upon meeting. Their second encounter doesn't go a lot better.

Judge is loving the challenge. Chloe is everything he doesn't want in a woman, but he can't stop finding ways to spend time with her. He knows she's dealing with loss and change.

He just doesn't know how deep that goes. Or how ingrained it is for Chloe to care for those who have a place in her heart, how hard it will be to trust anyone to look after her...

And how much harder it is when it's his turn.

Taking the Leap: A River Rain Novel, Book 3

Alexandra Sharp has been crushing on her co-worker, John "Rix" Hendrix for years. He's her perfect man, she knows it.

She's just not his perfect woman, and she knows that too.

Then Rix gives Alex a hint that maybe there's a spark between them that, if she takes the leap, she might be able to fan into a flame This leads to a crash and burn, and that's all shy Alex needs to catch the hint never to take the risk again.

However, with undeniable timing, Rix's ex, who broke his heart, and Alex's family, who spent her lifetime breaking hers, rear their heads, gearing up to offer more drama. With the help of some match-making friends, Rix and Alex decide to face the onslaught together...

As a fake couple.

Making the Match, A River Rain Novel, Book 4

Decades ago, tennis superstar Tom Pierce and "It Girl" Mika Stowe met at a party.

Mika fell in love. Tom was already in love with his wife. As badly as Tom wanted Mika as a friend, Mika knew it would hurt too much to be attracted to this amazing man and never be able to have him.

They parted ways for what they thought would be forever, only to reconnect just once, when unspeakable tragedy darkens Mika's life.

Years later, the impossible happens.

A time comes when they're both unattached.

But now Tom has made a terrible mistake. A mistake so damaging to the ones he loves, he feels he'll never be redeemed.

Mika has never forgotten how far and how fast she fell when she met him, but Tom's transgression is holding her distant from reaching out.

There are matchmakers in their midst, however.

And when the plot has been unleashed to make that match, Tom and Mika are thrown into an international intrigue that pits them against a Goliath of the sports industry.

Now they face a massive battle at the same time they're navigating friendship, attraction, love, family, grief, redemption, two very different lives lived on two opposite sides of a continent and a box full of kittens.

Fighting the Pull, A River Rain Novel, Book 5

Hale Wheeler inherited billions from his father. He's decided to take those resources and change the world for the better. He's married to his mission, so he doesn't have time for love.

There's more lurking behind this decision. He hasn't faced the tragic loss of his father, or the bitterness of his parents' divorce. He doesn't intend to follow in his father's footsteps, breaking a woman's heart in a way it will never mend. So he vows he'll never marry.

But Hale is intrigued when he meets Elsa Cohen, the ambitious celebrity news journalist who has been reporting on his famous family. He warns her off, but she makes him a deal. She'll pull back in exchange for an exclusive interview.

Elsa Cohen is married to her career, but she wants love, marriage, children. She also wants the impossibly handsome, fiercely loyal, tenderhearted Hale Wheeler.

They go head-to-head, both denying why there are fireworks every time they meet. But once they understand their undeniable attraction, Elsa can't help but fall for the dynamic do-gooder.

As for Hale, he knows he needs to fight the pull of the beautiful, bold, loving Elsa Cohen, because breaking her would crush him.

ROCK CHICK REMATCH: A ROCK CHICK NOVELLA

COMING JANUARY 23, 2024

New York Times and *USA Today* bestselling author Kristen Ashley brings a new story in her Rock Chick series...

In high school, Malia Clark found the man of her dreams.

Darius Tucker.

But life hits them full in the face way before it ever should. Darius makes a drastic decision to keep his family safe and Malia leaves town with a secret.

When Malia returns, she seeks Darius to share all, but Darius finds out before she can tell him. At the same time, she finds out just how much Darius has changed in the years she's been away.

She just refuses to give up on him.

Until he forces her hand.

Secrets come between Malia and Darius, at the same time Malia has to worry about weird things going on at the law firm where she works, her kid wants a car and she's stuck in slow-cooker hell. Luckily, her ride or dies have her back.

And in the meantime, she might just learn she never should have lost hope in Darius Tucker.

DISCOVER MORE KRISTEN ASHLEY

GOSSAMER IN THE DARKNESS:
A Fantasyland Novella

Their engagement was set when they were children. Loren Copeland, the rich and handsome Marquess of Remington, would marry Maxine Dawes, the stunning daughter of the Count of Derryman. It's a power match. The perfect alliance for each house.

However, the Count has been keeping secret a childhood injury that means Maxine can never marry. He's done this as he searches for a miracle so this marriage can take place. He needs the influence such an alliance would give him, and he'll stop at nothing to have it.

The time has come. There could be no more excuses. No more delays. The marriage has to happen, or the contract will be broken.

When all seems lost, the Count finds his miracle: There's a parallel universe where his daughter has a twin. He must find her, bring her to his world and force her to make the Marquess fall in love with her.

And this, he does.

WILD WIND: A Chaos Novella

When he was sixteen years old, Jagger Black laid eyes on the girl who was his. At a cemetery. During her mother's funeral.

For years, their lives cross, they feel the pull of their connection, but then they go their separate ways.

But when Jagger sees that girl chasing someone down the street, he doesn't think twice before he wades right in. And when he gets a full-on dose of the woman she's become, he knows he finally has to decide if he's all in or if it's time to cut her loose.

She's ready to be cut loose.

But Jagger is all in.

DREAM BITES COOKBOOK:
Cooking with the Commandos
Short Stories by Kristen Ashley
Recipes by Suzanne M. Johnson

From *New York Times* bestseller Kristen Ashley and *USA Today* bestseller Suzanne M. Johnson...

See what's cooking!

You're invited to Denver and into the kitchens of Hawk Delgado's commandos: Daniel "Mag" Magnusson, Boone Sadler, Axl Pantera and Augustus "Auggie" Hero as they share with you some of the goodness they whip up for their women.

Not only will you get to spend time with the commandos, the Dream Team makes an appearance with their men, and there are a number of special guest stars. It doesn't end there, you'll also find some bonus recipes from a surprise source who doesn't like to be left out.

So strap in for a trip to Denver, a few short stories, some reminiscing and a lot of great food.

(Half of the proceeds of this cookbook go to the Rock Chick Nation Charities)

Welcome to Dream Bites, Cooking with the Commandos!

WILD FIRE: A Chaos Novella

"You know you can't keep a good brother down."

The Chaos Motorcycle Club has won its war. But not every brother rode into the sunset with his woman on the back of his bike.

Chaos returns with the story of Dutch Black, a man whose father was the moral compass of the Club, until he was murdered. And the man who raised Dutch protected the Club at all costs. That combination is the man Dutch is intent on becoming.

It's also the man that Dutch is going to go all out to give to his woman.

QUIET MAN: A Dream Man Novella

Charlotte "Lottie" McAlister is in the zone. She's ready to take on the next chapter of her life, and since she doesn't have a man, she'll do what she's done all along. She'll take care of business on her own. Even if that business means starting a family.

The problem is, Lottie has a stalker. The really bad kind. The kind that means she needs a bodyguard.

Enter Mo Morrison.

Enormous. Scary.

Quiet.

Mo doesn't say much, and Lottie's used to getting attention. And she wants Mo's attention. Badly.

But Mo has a strict rule. If he's guarding your body, that's all he's doing with it.

However, the longer Mo has to keep Lottie safe, the faster he falls for the beautiful blonde who has it so together, she might even be able to tackle the demons he's got in his head that just won't die.

But in the end, Lottie and Mo don't only have to find some way to keep hands off until the threat is over, they have to negotiate the over-protective Hot Bunch, Lottie's crazy stepdad, Tex, Mo's crew of frat-boy commandos, not to mention his nutty sisters.

All before Lottie finally gets her Dream Man.

And Mo can lay claim to his Dream Girl.

ROUGH RIDE: A Chaos Novella

Rosalie Holloway put it all on the line for the Chaos Motorcycle Club.

Informing to Chaos on their rival club—her man's club, Bounty—Rosalie knows the stakes. And she pays them when her man, who she was hoping to scare straight, finds out she's betrayed him and he delivers her to his brothers to mete out their form of justice.

But really, Rosie has long been denying that, as she drifted away from her Bounty, she's been falling in love with Everett "Snapper" Kavanagh, a Chaos brother. Snap is the biker-boy-next door with the snowy blue eyes, quiet confidence and sweet disposition who was supposed to keep her safe...and fell down on that job.

For Snapper, it's always been Rosalie, from the first time he saw her at the Chaos Compound. He's just been waiting for a clear shot. But he didn't want to get it after his Rosie was left bleeding, beat down and broken by Bounty on a cement warehouse floor.

With Rosalie a casualty of an ongoing war, Snapper has to guide her to trust him, take a shot with him, build a them...

And fold his woman firmly in the family that is Chaos.

ROCK CHICK REAWAKENING:
A Rock Chick Novella

From *New York Times* bestselling author, Kristen Ashley, comes the long-awaited story of Daisy and Marcus, *Rock Chick Reawakening*. A prequel to Kristen's *Rock Chick* series, *Rock Chick Reawakening* shares the tale of the devastating event that nearly broke Daisy, an event that set Marcus Sloane—one of Denver's most respected businessmen and one of the Denver underground's most feared crime bosses—into finally making his move to win the heart of the woman who stole his.

DISCOVER 1001 DARK NIGHTS COLLECTION TEN

DRAGON LOVER by Donna Grant
A Dragon Kings Novella

KEEPING YOU by Aurora Rose Reynolds
An Until Him/Her Novella

HAPPILY EVER NEVER by Carrie Ann Ryan
A Montgomery Ink Legacy Novella

DESTINED FOR ME by Corinne Michaels
A Come Back for Me/Say You'll Stay Crossover

MADAM ALANA by Audrey Carlan
A Marriage Auction Novella

DIRTY FILTHY BILLIONAIRE by Laurelin Paige
A Dirty Universe Novella

HIDE AND SEEK by Laura Kaye
A Blasphemy Novella

TANGLED WITH YOU by J. Kenner
A Stark Security Novella

TEMPTED by Lexi Blake
A Masters and Mercenaries Novella

THE DANDELION DIARY by Devney Perry
A Maysen Jar Novella

CHERRY LANE by Kristen Proby
A Huckleberry Bay Novella

THE GRAVE ROBBER by Darynda Jones
A Charley Davidson Novella

CRY OF THE BANSHEE by Heather Graham
A Krewe of Hunters Novella

DARKEST NEED by Rachel Van Dyken
A Dark Ones Novella

CHRISTMAS IN CAPE MAY by Jennifer Probst
A Sunshine Sisters Novella

A VAMPIRE'S MATE by Rebecca Zanetti
A Dark Protectors/Rebels Novella

WHERE IT BEGINS by Helena Hunting
A Pucked Novella

Also from Blue Box Press

THE MARRIAGE AUCTION by Audrey Carlan
Season One, Volume One
Season One, Volume Two

Season One, Volume Three
Season One, Volume Four

THE JEWELER OF STOLEN DREAMS by M.J. Rose

SAPPHIRE STORM by Christopher Rice writing as C. Travis Rice
A Sapphire Cove Novel

ATLAS: THE STORY OF PA SALT by Lucinda Riley and Harry
Whittaker

LOVE ON THE BYLINE by Xio Axelrod
A Plays and Players Novel

A SOUL OF ASH AND BLOOD by Jennifer L. Armentrout
A Blood and Ash Novel

START US UP by Lexi Blake
A Park Avenue Promise Novel

FIGHTING THE PULL by Kristen Ashley
A River Rain Novel

VISIONS OF FLESH AND BLOOD by Jennifer L. Armentrout and
Rayvn Salvador
A Blood and Ash/Flesh and Fire Compendium

A FIRE IN THE FLESH by Jennifer L. Armentrout
A Flesh and Fire Novel

ON BEHALF OF BLUE BOX PRESS,

LIZ BERRY, M.J. ROSE, AND JILLIAN STEIN
WOULD LIKE TO THANK ~

Steve Berry
Doug Scofield
Benjamin Stein
Kim Guidroz
Tanaka Kangara
Stacey Tardif
Asha Hossain
Chris Graham
Jessica Saunders
Kate Boggs
Donna Perry
Richard Blake
and Simon Lipskar

Daisy & Marcus
Greed & Sylvie

Made in United States
North Haven, CT
06 July 2024

54466241R00086